Colonization: Book One of Paradise Reclaimed

Aubrie Dionne

Colonization: Book One of Paradise Reclaimed

Copyright © 2012 Aubrie Dionne

All rights reserved.

ISBN: 0985148373
ISBN-13 (print): 978-0-9851483-7-9
ISBN-13 (ebook): 978-0-9856562-0-1

Inkspell Publishing

18, Scott Court, C-4

Ridgefield Park

07660 NJ

Edited By Rie Langdon.

Cover art By Najla Qamber

DEDICATION

To everyone out there looking for their home...

ACKNOWLEDGMENTS

There are so many people who have helped and supported me in this project and over the years! First of all, I'd like to thank my agent, Dawn Dowdle, for believing in my work. Next, Shilpa Mudiganti for taking on a book that doesn't fit in the mainstream YA that you see on the shelves today. My fantastic cover designer, Najla Qamber, comes next for creating a cover that represents exactly what this book is about. I'd like to thank my editor, Rie Langdon and my publicist, Majanka Verstraete, and the entire team at Inkspell publishing. Thank you to my critique partners, Cherie Reich, Theresa Milstein, and Cher Green for all of your wise advice. My mom, Joanne, and my sister Brianne are my biggest supporters, and I want to thank you, too. I want to thank the person that has had the biggest influence in my professional life, my flute teacher, Peggy Vagts, for teaching me so much more than Bach Sonatas. Lastly, my husband Chris for putting up with all my crazy ideas.

CHAPTER ONE

PREDESTINED

"I'm telling you, Andromeda, you're the one." Great-grandma Tiff grinned from the halo of her sleep pod. Her eyes sparkled like two winking stars.

"I can't even pass the colonization pretests." I squirmed on the edge, about to fall on the floor. Whenever she alluded to her psychic powers and me as the savior of the colony, my stomach bubbled up acid and I thought I'd spew all over the wallscreen.

Luckily, I knew how to distract her. "Tell me again about the pirate space station and how you convinced Grandpapa to keep you on the New Dawn."
She smiled softly and waved her hand at me, rustling the tubes connected to her arms.

"I didn't convince him. He convinced me. Besides, being a space pirate isn't what it's cracked up to be. The space station stank worse than the filth oozing beneath the biodome. I slept against the generators to keep from shivering, with one eye open every night. There were no Guide-driven objectives, and lawlessness was everywhere."
I closed my eyes and tried to imagine a world without the Guide, a world without rules. Fear rushed in, followed by enough curiosity to keep me listening. "And?"

Tiff cleared her throat. "When I left, the whole place was in ruins, and I couldn't imagine eating more of that recycled food."

I wrinkled my nose. Recycled food sounded nasty.

"You were lucky to be born on the ship, my dear, and even luckier to be the generation reaching the paradise planet."

"I don't want to leave the New Dawn." Embarrassed by the edge in my voice, I bit my lip, offering an apologetic smile. "We have everything here we could ever need."

"Change is the only constant in our lives. It shapes us as much as it tears us down. You're destined for wonderful things, Andromeda, and you can either fight the rising tide or ride it out to sea."

Thinking of the future reminded me of swimming in the deeper end of the aerobics pool on accelerated mode: constantly struggling and never getting anywhere. "Can't we talk about something else?"

Tiff sighed, her shaky fingers drumming on the plastic rim of the sleep pod. She couldn't move much else, and I wondered if she sometimes felt imprisoned in her own body. I couldn't imagine living for over three hundred years.

"That's enough for now, my dear. Besides, there's a boy waiting to see you at the portal."

"I don't see anyone hailing the wallscreen."

She settled back into her sleep pod and pressed a button on the side. The lid descended slowly and I ducked out of the way. "Don't stay out too late or your mother will worry."

"I'm not going anywhere. I have too much studying to do."

Her crackly voice echoed within the plastic cocoon. "Someday you'll believe me."

As the lid sealed, the wallscreen beeped and displayed the one face I could stare at all day.

"Sirius, what are you doing here? It's almost curfew."

I stepped around the gurgling machine that kept Great-grandma Tiff alive, careful not to tangle my legs in the wires and tubes.

He smiled, a devilish grin teasing me and luring me in at the same time. My logical mind disintegrated into irrational cravings. "Come on. I have something I know you'll want to see."

I pressed the button on the front panel and the portal dematerialized between us in a million swirling specks. He leaned against the chrome wall, half his face covered by his wavy black-as-deep-space hair. Eagerness tingled inside me and I squashed it down, trying to look annoyed.

"What is it?"

He brushed a lock of hair from his face and his dark eyes gleamed. "It's a surprise."

I pretended to consider staying. "I've got a lot of work to do."

"Trust me. You'll be glad you came with me."

"Oh, all right. As long as I'm back by curfew."

He grabbed my hand, and electricity sizzled between us. His voice turned low and velvety. "You may not want to be back at all."

I followed him down the corridor, wondering how my lanky best friend had turned into an out-of-this-galaxy hottie. I couldn't pinpoint the day my feelings had changed. They'd rushed up whenever we spent time together and I had to swallow them down because we'd reached our seventeenth year.

He spoke over his shoulder as he led me to the elevator. "I overheard the bioteam talking today."

"We're not going to the biodome, are we?"

"Yup. Don't worry. It's not the part your mom works in. We're breaking into the livestock cells."

The thought of smelly goats and cows drove my romantic thoughts away. "Why, in all the vastness of space, are we going there?"

The elevator beeped, and the door dematerialized. He

raised an eyebrow, teasing me with his pouty, kissable lips. "You'll see."

We seemed too old for these adventures, but I couldn't turn him down.

As we stepped onto the biodome level, the musky scent of fur and animal droppings hung heavy in the air.

"I'm not walking through the goat pen."

He laughed and squeezed my hand. "You won't have to."

We crouched beneath the glass panels, making sure all of the biologists had left for the night. I squinted in the dim light. As they sensed our presence, the bleats of animals echoed from the cells beside us.

Sirius led me past the livestock to the exotic animals in the back. He positioned himself in front of a cell with a warning sign blinking across it.

"The desert cows from Sahara 354? Are you crazy?"

He held up a thin card, looking way too amused. "I stole the key."

"I'm not going in there. They could stomp us to death."

Before I could grab his arm, he'd already swiped the card and slipped into the cell.

"Sirius, wait!"

I cringed as I entered the darkness, preparing for a foot the size of a table to squash me or a trunk to smack me against the wall. All was quiet.

"Annie, come closer."

A small lump crept out of the shadows, and my heart melted. A tiny three-trunked calf waddled over to Sirius. He crouched down and pulled miniature carrots from his pockets.

I fell to my knees beside the animal. "What a cutie!"

"It was born this morning. They've segregated the newborn to keep it safe from the others."

I ran my hand over the soft newly-formed hide. Pity panged inside me. It was cruel to keep it here, down in a dark cell in the emptiness of deep space. The calf should be enjoying the vast desert of Sahara 354, basking in real sunlight with sand under its toes and the breeze on its back.

"They should have left the desert cows alone. They're not even from Old Earth."

A trunk swung at his head, and Sirius ducked. He fed the calf another carrot. "From what I've researched, Sahara 354 had two suns, one of them about to go supernova. This was the only chance they had." He handed me the rest of the carrots. "Go on. You try."

Bending down, I pulled a carrot from the bunch and offered it to the newborn. The calf approached me hesitantly, nibbling on the end. Innocence and fear shone in its black eye. "So they're like us, refugees from a dying planet."

Sirius shrugged my concern away. "Guess so."

"I wonder how they survived three generations on the ship, away from their home?"

"Don't you remember the section on genetics?" I thought back, but all my classes ran together. I must have been daydreaming again. "Remind me."

"Sure. You'll have to review it before the tests."

"Like I have any time to study with you parading me around."

"Sheesh, Annie. Next time I'll go alone." Sirius sat down and crossed his legs. The calf crooned like a child watching its parents fight. I placed my hand on the animal's head to comfort it, thinking of a way to apologize to Sirius. It wasn't his fault I wasn't prepared for the tests, and I loved going out with him any chance I got.

"No, Sirius. I'm sorry, okay? I'm enjoying myself. I really am. It's just the tests are coming up and I've been such a slacker."

He sighed, throwing a piece of hay over his shoulder. "You'll do fine."

His voice sounded so sure of it, I wondered if he

thought my relationship to the commander would sway the results. A current of anger rose up and I exhaled, calming myself. No, Sirius wouldn't think of me as a cheat. Surely the tests were fair.

"So how did these animals survive?"

Sirius reached over to pet the calf and his hand brushed mine, igniting heat that traveled from my fingers to my chest. Does he feel it, too? If so, his face remained impassive, reminding me of Ms. Hoodcroft spouting from her miniscreen text.

"The biologists took the strongest ones to start a population. They controlled their breeding mates to ensure each generation had optimal genes and no inbreeding, to avoid recessive or deleterious traits."

Realization hit me and I whispered, "Just like us."

"Yup."

I dropped the rest of the carrots on the floor and the calf knelt to gobble them up.

Sirius turned to me. "Annie, what's wrong?"

The question came from nowhere and everywhere. It had hung between us for as long as I could remember, becoming the one unknown dominating my life. I finally asked what I'd been wondering, hoping. "Do you think we'll be paired together?"

Sirius's eyes were dark oceans of mystery. He blinked and shrugged. "We'll worry about that when the time comes. For now, let's enjoy ourselves."

Sirius's locator beeped and panic zapped through me. "What time is it?"

He gave me a charming, apologetic smile. "Past curfew."

"Damn." My fingers fumbled as I reinserted the energy cell. Ten messages. I was so dead. Like, sucked-into-a-black-hole dead.

I raised my arm and my mother's face stared back at me, crinkled up in anger. "Andromeda! Where are you? Your locator's turned off."

I winced, making sure Sirius and the baby calf didn't show on the screen. "I took a break from studying. I'll be home soon."

"You'd better." Her voice changed from furious to vulnerable in two words. "Great-grandma Tiff is gone."

CHAPTER TWO

LULLABY

The funeral came days before the speck of Paradise 21 glimmered on the horizon. I stood next to Mom and Dad in front of Great-grandma Tiff's casket, wondering why she couldn't have lived just a few more days to see our new home planet for herself. But Tiff didn't do anything she didn't want to do. Maybe she hadn't wanted to see it.

"Andromeda, stop sniffling and keep your head up." Mom tugged on my arm and handed me a microfiber cloth from her pocket. She didn't want me making a scene in front of the congregation.

A speaker took the platform, silencing any sort of smart reply I had stored up for her nitpicking.

"We're gathered here today to honor the memory of Tiffany Barliss."

Ten words in, and the man had already infuriated me. No one called her Tiffany. Her name was Great-grandma Tiff. He spoke of how my great-grandma came to the New Dawn with the space pirates, the same year the legendary Aries Ryder went crazy and gave the pirates the location of the ship's trajectory. Great-grandma Tiff's ship came to capture Aries, and she ended up staying in her place.

The   speaker   babbled   on   about   the   many

9

accomplishments in Great-grandma Tiff's life as my attention wandered. I stared off into the space panel above our heads. The stars blew by, strands of diamonds streaking through a sea of darkness. I imagined soaring above the congregation like a bird from Old Earth. Space wasn't a dark, vacuous void, but a warm and glimmering night sky with a mild breeze buoying me up. The illusion comforted me from the harsh truth. We lived in a pocket of recycled air with nothing all around, waiting to suck us out.

The ceremony ended and I ran my hand along the white nanofiber plastic of her closed coffin, the only material we could afford to discard. The lid felt cool and slick to my touch, and I wondered if her body was cold as well. Deep space, as I'd been told, was three degrees above absolute zero, the temperature at which molecules stopped moving. Repressing a shiver, I let go as Mom pulled me away.

With the push of a button, the operations supervisor ejected her casket into space. I watched the rectangular box grow smaller and smaller until I squinted my eyes and nothing remained. I imagined my great-grandma's body floating for eternity into the vast unknown, and the hairs rose on the back of my neck. I turned to Mom. "Why couldn't we bring her with us to Paradise 21?"

Mom's mouth set in a grim line and her eyes told me not to ask such questions in public. "The ceremony is a tradition. It's been this way ever since the New Dawn left Old Earth."

"She would have wanted to come."

Mom ignored my comment and kissed my cheek. "I'm going to cut through the crowd to talk to your grandpapa. Please stay out of trouble."

"Okay." She might as well have told me to find something better to do for the rest of the day. The line of people surrounding my grandpapa's hoverchair was as long as the line of people waiting to get off the ship. He was, after all, the commander, and the most important person alive.

At three hundred fifty-seven, my grandpapa had seen more years than anyone on board and was the only man old enough to have known the previous commander, who knew the very first lifers on the New Dawn. The two of them spanned eight generations altogether. Sometimes grandpapa's importance worked in my favor, because our family had all the luxuries the ship could offer, but today it just made life worse. Everyone paid attention to us, and I had to make sure to behave as the commander's granddaughter should.

"Sorry, Annie."

I turned. Sirius's intense brown eyes flustered me, making me feel as if we were the only two people in the room. He put his hand on my shoulder and the warmth of his skin burned through my white uniform. I wanted to press myself against him like I'd seen lifemates do, but we weren't supposed to have favorites.

I stared at his hand touching me and glanced back at him, raising an eyebrow. His cheeks flushed and he pulled away. I shrugged his apology off. "She wasn't supposed to live that long, anyway. You know they only kept her alive because of my grandpapa."

Sirius flared his eyes to warn me to stop, but the whole day had frayed at my nerves. I couldn't help all the feelings rushing out. My world was changing around me and all I wanted was for it to stay the same. Tears blurred my vision and I turned away, embarrassed.

"Come on. Follow me."

Sirius put a gentle hand on my shoulder and led me out of the room into the quiet corridor. He put his arm around me and pulled me close against his hard chest. I smelled the soap he'd used that morning mingling with his own heady scent.

"I'll take you back to your room, okay?"

"That's not necessary." Dad ruined the moment, as if

the funeral couldn't ruin the day enough.

He must have followed us into the corridor. Were my forbidden feelings that easy to see?

Dad smiled at Sirius, but his mouth tightened in the corners. "I'm going back to work, and I have to stop by our family unit to get my tools."

"Yes, sir." Sirius nodded and stepped away, letting me go. His hand lingered on the curve of my back before he turned to my father. "Sorry for your loss."

Dad's voice was cold. "Thank you, son." With a nod, he dismissed Sirius and turned to me. "Come now, Andromeda. You have studying to do for your colonization testing."

I allowed myself one backward glance at the blank window of space where my great-grandma's casket drifted off, before following him down the corridor. I hoped he'd leave me alone, but Dad was in a lecturing mood.

"These exams are the most important tests you'll take over the course of your life. They'll determine your future job assignment in the colony. Whether you'll be a housekeeper, a planter, or even a systems operator. It would behoove you to do well."

Dad only pushed me because he cared, but I couldn't bring myself to take the tests seriously. They forced me to accept the reality of Paradise 21, and I wasn't ready to grow up. The tests had seemed so far away, but all of a sudden they hung over my head. I couldn't cram in all I'd missed during the years I'd slacked off.

I told him what he wanted to hear. "Yes, Dad. I'll try."

He opened his mouth, probably to lecture me more, when the ship lurched, slamming us into the wall. I banged my elbow against the chrome, sending a sting up my arm. As Dad helped me stand, the lights flickered off and dim-red emergency ones flashed on. The familiar chug of the generators underneath my feet stopped, and the ship felt oddly motionless. An alarm wailed.

"It's the engines." Dad grabbed my arm and pulled me

forward. "I have to get to the lower decks."

We reached our family unit and he threw his electrolytic capacitor into a plastic container. "Stay here." His voice sounded authoritative, but a glimmer of fear crossed his eyes.

I nodded and watched him sprint down the corridor until the portal re-materialized, static particles solidifying, leaving me alone in my family unit.

What if the engines failed before we reached Paradise 21? Part of me relished the idea. We'd live on the ship our whole lives, like our ancestors before us. We wouldn't have to worry about atmospheric conditions, threatening species, or building cities on the foamy stuff they called turf. Then I realized we'd be adrift in space with Great-grandma Tiff. We'd lose power and our resources would dwindle even further. We'd run out of food. What if the heat stopped working and we froze to death?

That thought scared me more than living on Paradise 21. I had to do something. Hefting my backpack, I pressed the portal panel and jumped up and down until the particles dematerialized. I'd never been as low as the engine decks, but I had an idea where Dad worked. Following in his footsteps, I wiggled my way through people rushing down the corridor, and pressed the elevator panel.

"Annie, where are you going?"

Sirius caught me red-handed. With my pack on my back and my hand on the elevator panel, I looked like crazy Aries Ryder heading for the escape pods.

"I was just...going to..." I stammered and looked down until I remembered he wasn't where he should be either. "Why are you here?"

"I came to check on you. After you left, Commander Barliss lost consciousness. One minute he was talking to all the people onboard, and the next his eyes were shut."

My heart fluttered at the same pace as the flashing lights. Too many things were going wrong all in one day.

My world was disintegrating before my eyes. "Is he going to be all right?"

"I heard the medics talking as they took him to the hospital deck. The ship is faltering without his mind to steer it forward. The engines are sputtering out."

The elevator portal dematerialized and I rushed in. Sirius slid in next to me, and the platform took off down to the lower decks.

"Where's the elevator headed?"

I flicked my eyes up, daring him to stop me. "The engine room. I want to help."

He slammed his fist on the portal jam button and the elevator stopped between decks, jerking us both. I fell against him, and he held me in his arms. "You can't do anything down there. It's dangerous, and you might get hurt."

I squirmed away and stared him straight in the eyes, pleading. "I have to do something."

"Let's go to the hospital deck and see your grandpapa. He's the key to saving the ship. If he dies, we're all lost." Sirius put an encouraging hand on my arm. He apparently had more faith in me than I had in myself, and his unwavering esteem unnerved me. Emotions I shouldn't feel welled up inside me, threatening to break past my lips. I wanted to tell him how much he meant to me, how much I wanted us to be together, but Sirius saved me from confessing. "If anyone can save him, you can."

"I'll try."

He pressed the panel for the upper decks, and the elevator took off in the opposite direction. I hoped Dad was safe in the engine room. Many lifers died in accidents caused by the combustion chambers.

Dizziness overtook me, and an invisible force detached my feet from the floor. I clutched Sirius's arm. "What's happening?"

"I bet the gravity rings are failing."

My stomach heaved and I swallowed a lump in my

throat. An eternity passed before the elevator portal dematerialized and we stood before the hospital deck. The dim glow of the emergency lights lit our path as we ran to the medical bay, my feet bouncing high in the light gravity. Colonists guarded the portal, but they recognized me and let us through without questions. As Commander Barliss's great-granddaughter, I was accustomed to getting my way.

My grandpapa lay in a real bed, one of those platforms raised up from the floor with paper-thin sheets like in the pictures from Old Earth. If they were going to use real fabric to comfort him, then it had to be bad. The numerous wires running from his arms and input devices in his head didn't faze me. Those were normal. The scurrying nurses made me nervous.

"What's wrong with him?" I walked over to his bed and took his veiny hand in my own. His bones were light as laser sticks and his skin felt so brittle and thin I feared it would flake off under my touch.

"The funeral put too much stress on his heart." The head nurse appeared to be about my mother's age, with gray streaks of hair. "He's lost consciousness and none of our stimulants have been effective."

I turned to Sirius, and he nodded as if I knew what to do. "Just talk to him, say something to cheer him up." Around us, small glass vials floated in the air as the gravity rings cycled down. I gripped the metal bed handles to keep from floating away. At least they'd strapped my grandpapa down.

"Can you hear me?" I tried to block out my surroundings, the shouting from the corridor, the emergency wail, the floating utensils, even Sirius's proximity, and focused on my grandpapa. His skin sagged into sunken cheeks and his bones looked fragile compared to the sturdy metal wires connecting him to the mainframe.

I don't know where the idea came from, but I opened my mouth and began to sing a song Great-grandma Tiff taught me, a song she'd learned from her mom and her mom before her—a song from Old Earth. My voice felt weak in my throat, and I broke the melody to take a deeper breath and support my stomach muscles. My singing ability was nothing special, but at least the swell of the melody came through.

I lost myself in the song, closing my eyes and picturing the words as places on Old Earth—city skyscrapers, radiant sun, tickling grass, and blue oceans—before overpopulation and wars over resources ruined everything. I reached back through time, borrowing images of the past. I wanted him to see something other than the inside of the ship. I wanted to give him hope.

Glass crashed around me. Cringing, I stopped singing and opened my eyes. Gravity had pulled the vials to the floor. The lights flashed on, and the emergency wail trailed off into silence.

"Tiff? Is that you?"

I looked down, and my grandpapa peered up at me with watery eyes. "No, Grandpapa. It's Andromeda."

He blinked twice and then seemed to focus and regain awareness of the room and the ship. "Oh, yes. I'm sorry. You resemble her, right down to the freckles on your nose. I seem to have lost it for a moment."

"Are you okay?" I leaned in. His skin was so pale I could see the thin blue veins underneath.

"Yes, yes, I'm fine." He sat up, and the tubes and wires pulled taut. "Get my hoverchair. I've got a lot of work left to do."

The nurses flooded around him and pushed me back. As always, my time with him was short. He was too important to bother with minor things. I slouched down. My arms were weights, pulling me to the floor. The song had drained all my energy.

Sirius took my hand in his. His skin warmed my cold fingertips as he wrapped his strong fingers around my small, pale hand.

"That was amazing, Annie."

I shrugged, embarrassed he had heard me sing. "I didn't know what else to do."

"What you did was perfect."

A woman cleared her throat and I whipped around. Some of the nurses stared at us, and I felt naked standing there holding Sirius's hand. I dropped it faster than a hot-energy capacitor. "Come on, we don't want to be in the way."

"Of course."

Even though we left my granddad alive and well, the truth burdened my heart. He wouldn't live forever, and soon enough we'd have to leave him on the New Dawn.

As we approached the elevator, Sirius whispered under his breath, "Why doesn't he appoint someone else to take his place? It seems dangerous to have an old man in charge of the entire ship."

"He doesn't want another person to be connected to the New Dawn." I pressed the panel and the elevator portal dematerialized, allowing us to step in. Chaos had cluttered the deck moments before, but now people walked about, doing their daily business, the red glow of the emergency lights just a memory. How easily they forget.

"Why not?" Sirius jammed his hands inside the pockets in his uniform. I thought of how he'd held my hand only moments ago, and the feeling of his fingers wrapping around mine. I wanted to grab one of his hands and see if the same rush of emotion came back again, but I turned and entered the elevator instead.

"Because whoever is connected can't join us on Paradise 21. He'd be stuck to the mainframe for the rest of his life. My grandpapa doesn't want anyone to have to share his fate, especially when we're this close. It would be a waste of a life. We'll need all of the young colonists to explore and build up the outpost."

"Why doesn't he at least train someone, in case he

doesn't make it?"

"It's useless." I shook my head. "If you connect to the mainframe too quickly, it can drive you crazy. It almost did to my grandpapa. He never wanted another man to go through what he did. He lost himself completely to the machine and came back forever altered. For that reason, the training procedures are time-consuming. By the time we reach Paradise 21, anyone he chooses would still be in the beginning of the transformation."

"Oh, I see." Sirius moved his shoulders as if a chill blew by his neck. "Let's hope we get there in time."

CHAPTER THREE

TESTS

Ms. Hoodcroft pressed a button and the main screen flashed with a picture of an impossibly large and radiant violet flower, taller than a man and bursting with white tentacles shooting outside its bell-shaped petals. It dwarfed one of the satellite probes taking pictures beside it. "Can anyone tell me what this is?"

We'd been fed information about plant species for months now, and every flower blended together in a vast bouquet. I scanned the classroom. Only one girl held up her hand.

"That's Trillium Bisonate." She ran a hand through her unbelievably perfect, long auburn locks. "Very poisonous, very deadly."

"Excellent, Nova."

I sighed, shifting my shoulders against my uncomfortable plastic seat. You'd think with a genetic matching program everyone would have an equal amount of brains and beauty, but Nova had them both in superfluous quantities. Her hair always flowed down her back in luscious waves and her uniform fit snugly in all the right places, bringing out her supple curves. I looked down at my own baggy pants and smoothed my stray wispy-blond ends, rolling my eyes.

Mrs. Hoodcraft scanned the rest of us in disappointment, tapping her fingertips on the image projector. "What will you do when you stumble across one of these, hmm? The tentacles will pull you into its stigma so the flower can digest you over the course of thirty days." The teacher's eyes narrowed as she pressed the button for the next image. "Now, how about this one?"

Sirius flicked his eyes over to catch my attention. I tried to ignore him but he kept staring, making my cheeks hot. I feared Mrs. Hoodcraft would see my rebellious inner thoughts. Nova had just answered another question, and the teacher was busy explaining the properties of a large fern. I typed a message on my keyboard. *What's up?*

His message flashed on my desk screen moments later. *Meet me after class. I want to show you something.*

Mrs. Hoodcraft shot a glance in my direction, and I straightened up. When her eyes shifted away, I typed *K.*

The tests came next, a slew of questions I could barely answer about physics, biology, architecture, and chemistry. I made up half my answers, my brain as empty as a used energy cell.

Dad's disapproving voice sounded in my head and guilt crept in. I should have studied harder. The reality of the situation blindsided me and I wondered if they'd make me a janitor, sweeping up the dying turf while Nova did exciting things like lead exploratory teams into the unknown.

A flash of remorse turned my stomach as I wondered if the computer would use the tests to pair us up as well. I'd be stuck with a dummy mate and Sirius would get someone smart and beautiful. I clenched my teeth, stifling the rising wave of anger and frustration building up in my chest. I wanted to stand up and scream, but instead I tried harder, exhausting my memory, pulling at any information I could recall. All of a sudden, I cared about my destiny and my lifemate pairing. Too bad the wake-up call had come too late.

After the examinations, we shuffled out of class single-file. I walked to the line but Nova cut me off, glancing down like I was an annoying cleaning droid. She stood five inches taller than me, dwarfing me as I trailed behind her, my eyes boring a hole into her back.

Sirius waited for me in the corridor. He tilted his head and his eyes had a look of triumph, like he'd aced his tests in less time than I'd botched mine. "How did you do?"

"Terrible." I hugged my laptop to my chest, trying to hide behind it. "I'll end up cleaning dead turf."

"Nonsense." He smiled, lighting a spark in my heart. "I'm sure you did fine."

I wanted to blot out the tests and how they'd ruin my future. I wanted to pretend my life would be the same as before and none of us would get our assignments for the new world. I searched for anything to stop talking about it. "What did you want to show me?"

The curve of his lips promised something wonderful. "You'll see."

I followed Sirius down the corridor to the elevator, and he pressed the button for one of the lower decks. His eyes sparkled dangerously, and I wondered what rules he'd have us breaking.

"We're not going to the engine room, are we?"

His smile was as dazzling as the diamond stars. "No, this is even better."

We got off on deck four, two decks above the engine room. Sirius pulled out a disc and inserted it into a portal. "I borrowed the ID card from my dad."

I followed him into a large ship bay that buzzed with activity. Mechanics wearing shield masks welded chrome plates onto large truck-like things with tires taller than me and Sirius put together. Sparks rained around them like fireworks.

"They're called Landrovers." Sirius pointed beyond the large machines to small winged compartments at the far end of the bay. Workers airbrushed the *New Dawn's* symbol—a ship cutting through waves in blue and red paint—on the silver-tipped wings. "Over there are Corsairs, small planes able to travel long distances for scouting missions."

"Wow." Acid bubbled up in my stomach and I swallowed it down. They had made all the preparations. We really were headed to another world.

My head reeled. I didn't want to be there, staring change right in the face, but Sirius beamed like a newborn sun and I couldn't spoil his moment. I was happy he wanted to share it with me. I faked excitement. "This is amazing."

He took my hand and squeezed it. "I want to be an aviator, Annie. I want to fly those Corsairs in the purple skies of Paradise 21."

"Sirius, you can't choose what you do, the computers—"

"I know, but I slanted my answers to tip the scales. I answered all of the questions concerning aerodynamics and physics correctly and chose poor answers for biology and chemistry."

His words shocked me into silence. I'd never thought about cheating on the tests.

"Will it work?"

He raised an eyebrow. "We'll see."

One of the men shot up from his work and shut off his power tool. "Hey, you kids over there. You're not supposed to be here."

Sirius's eyes went wide. "They've spotted us! Come on, Annie. Run."

My heart jump-started, thudding in my chest. Before they could scan our wrist locators, Sirius and I raced toward the exit.

Two men in shiny silver bodysuits blocked the corridor. Sirius zigzagged across the metal walkway to another exit. "Over here!"

He'd already pressed the portal panel, and the chrome materialized as I caught up. Men in welding masks hunted us down. Sirius pressed the panel, and the portal rematerialized behind us before they got through. It would take another minute for them to restart the cycle and follow us.

We disappeared around the bend of the corridor. I huffed worse than the first time I ran a mile on the indoor track. My athletic scores were low, and I'd barely passed with nine minutes and fifty-seven seconds.

Sirius gazed over his shoulder and whooped. Besides a flushed face bringing out the perfect bridge of his nose, he looked as though he'd had a grand time.

"Do you think they'll follow us?"

"Nah." He leaned against the sight panel, a blue nebula hanging like a cosmic painting behind us. "They have too much work to do to waste time on us."

We were the only people in the corridor, and the air thickened with static friction. He dropped his head next to mine, our foreheads almost touching. "What a great adventure, Annie."

He glanced down at my quivering lips. Was he going to kiss me?

We hung suspended for a small eternity. So many emotions swirled through me at once, I couldn't process all of them: excitement, elation, fear. My conscience murmured one word. *Forbidden.*

I pulled my head back before it was too late, feeling my heart tear. "You could have gotten us into trouble."

He took a deep breath, as if he tried to repress his own feelings as well. "Just wait until we reach Paradise 21."

Our destiny slapped me in the face. The truth was a wall between us. Our assignments loomed in our future and soon there'd be no more adventures. Not for the two of us, anyway. A hundred teens made up our graduating class and the possibility we'd be matched together was slim, especially after they computed my miserable test results. "I have to report back to my family unit. My parents are going to wonder where I am."

"Like you could go anywhere on a ship in deep space?" He sounded disappointed.

I almost turned around, but my head intervened with my heart. We were growing too close. He had a gravitational pull on me that only increased the more time I spent with him. I took my first steps down the corridor in agony, as if I were pulling apart two fused-together polarized molecules. The computer wouldn't take our chemistry into account. The analytics probably only considered unromantic information such as aptitude and genetic compatibility.

The intercom beeped and fizzled, and I heard my grandpapa's voice echo throughout the ship. "All colonists report to the main deck in the auditorium immediately. We'll be arriving sooner than planned and preparations must be made at once."

I stood there with wobbly legs, teetering alongside a great abyss. Sirius came up by my side and nudged my arm. "You heard the man. Let's go."

We followed a rush of people into the main auditorium, a bubble-shaped glass dome at the head of the ship. I lost Sirius in the commotion but didn't try to find him. We all had our assigned places, and his family sat all the way across the room.

As I walked to my parents' pew at the head of the congregation, I filed in behind Nova. She chatted with another girl from my class. I listened more out of boredom than curiosity, anything to get my mind off of Paradise 21. Besides, she was right in front of me, so how could I help overhearing?

"I'm sure it's about Paradise 21. I've been waiting for this day my entire life." Nova clutched her laptop to her chest as if it were a badge to show off. "When the computer calculates my test scores, I'll be rewarded."

"You've always been so diligent." The other girl sucked up to her as if Nova could choose her position instead of the computer.

"Yes, well, finally those of us who have worked hard will get what we deserve."

"You'll certainly get a high-ranking job," the other girl chimed in. "I can only hope that I—"

Nova raised a hand to silence her. "You'll be fine. I'm talking about people spoiled by their family connections, thinking the commander will hand them respected titles on a golden platter."

The other girl shook her head. "Who do you mean?"

The people behind me pressed me forward, and I almost bumped into Nova. As I recovered, clutching the side of one of the pews, her voice fell to a whisper. "Andromeda, of course. She slacks around without a care for her school work and expects her grandpapa to waste a high position on her. That's not how the system works."

Fury rose up inside me like vomit, and I wanted to pull out a chunk of her beautiful hair. She thought I was unworthy of being Commander Barliss's great-granddaughter and that I ran around asking for favors all the time.

Suddenly the day seemed too much for me, the room full of people, the change in plans, Sirius's lips so close to mine. A wave of doubt overwhelmed me, and the room swooped in my eyes. Maybe she was right. I dreaded the arrival of Paradise 21 as much as Nova yearned for it. I didn't deserve all of the special attention and I certainly didn't live up to my family's name by being a mediocre student.

I took my seat next to my parents, sinking onto the plastic bench in shame. My mom was still dressed in her lab coat. She must have come right from the biodome, and oil and grease covered Dad's hands and arms.

To add the icing on an already stinking cake, Dad bent around Mom and asked me, "How were the tests?"

I bit back a negative retort. "Fine."

"You answered all the questions correctly?"

"As many as I could."

As the remaining colonists filtered in, my grandpapa appeared in the far rear of the auditorium. People clapped as he rode his hoverchair to the stage, haloed by the cloud of the cerulean nebula with stars on all sides. My heart trembled with regret as I saw him. I had achieved nothing for him to be proud of, nothing to aid in his mission: the New Dawn's quest. I thought of Great-grandma Tiff. It had only been a few days since she passed away, but I missed her severely. I'd lost the woman who believed in me, the only person who knew my secrets.

With a flick of his fingertips, my grandpapa pressed the panel on the armrest of the chair and his voice boomed out over the masses.

"Congratulations are in order. Paradise 21 is in sight."

The room erupted in shouts and applause. My grandpapa pointed to the glass behind him. One star sparkled brighter than all the rest, winking at me from beyond. As the ship sped toward it, the engines surged, rumbling in my gut like the voice of inevitability. The glimmering speck was no star. I stood up out of my seat. My eyes opened so wide they dried out and tears stung.

Commander Barliss hailed Paradise 21.

CHAPTER FOUR

ASSIGNMENTS

The food congealizer buzzed and gurgled as I dropped crushed tomatoes into the blades.

"I'll need that paste soon." Mom stirred a pot of boiling water, brewing up one of her great stew concoctions.

"It's almost ready." I pushed the button and watched the chunks turn to mush.

"It's too bad we lost the last crop of green beans." She threw in a dash of salt. "They would have added a nice touch."

"It's not your fault, Mom." Mold had infested the seeds, contaminating the entire container. As the chief microbiologist, any mistake like that weighed heavily on her shoulders.

She sighed, slumping forward. "Our stocks are low, and a lot of the seedlings aren't growing to full capacity." I poked the tomatoes on the countertop with a fork. They were smaller than my palm, with shriveled skin. Not too appetizing. Then again, I'd only seen healthy tomatoes in pictures from my history books of Old Earth.

"These look fine, Mom."

"We'll have much more to work with when we get to

Paradise 21: new soil, new species." Her face brightened while I frowned, turning back to the accumulating tomato paste. Was I the only one that didn't want to land?

The wallscreen beeped behind us and flashed the words *Incoming Message*. Mom took up my job at the food congealizer. "Go see what it is, honey."

I jogged into the family room and clicked on the main screen. As I read the words, I froze. *Life Assignments for Class Omega*.

Oh, no. When my grandpapa had announced they'd be speeding everything up at the meeting last night, I didn't think it'd be the next day. My insides tightened and I felt sick and goose-bumpy all at once. Half of me wanted to run into my room and hide, and the other half yearned to get it over with and press the damn button.

The food congealizer paused. "What's taking so long, Andromeda?"

"Nothing, Mom. I'll be right back."

I didn't want to share this moment with anyone. I couldn't handle the shame and humiliation of being assigned a less-than-adequate job and an ill-matched lifemate. I hoped I did better than I assumed on the tests, but I lived in denial of a lot of things.

They used to hand out the assignments on beautiful thick white paper, but that ran out two generations ago. Now all we had was a public screen available for everyone to see. I guess they figured we'd all know in a matter of days anyway. My mom wouldn't stay in the kitchen forever, so I gathered up my last smidgen of courage and pressed the button.

A long list of names flashed up. After a moment of panic, I realized it was in alphabetical order and scrolled down to the Bs. Next to my name it read *Agriculture, Section 34a: New Species Integration*. Relief flooded over me like a cool shower. Having a job with mom wasn't so bad. All those nights I'd listened to her complain about soil nutrients and growth cycles must have paid off. I was a much lower rank than she was, but I could always work my way up the system.

I scrolled down to see that Nova did indeed receive *Expedition Team Leader*, a highly coveted title, and Sirius earned *Navigator, First Officer*. My heart swelled. He did it. He'd manipulated the tests to be an aviator. I was so happy for him that for a moment I forgot all about the other part of our assignments: our lifemates.

I summoned the courage to scroll down. So far, I was content. If the job turned out okay, maybe the assignment would make me happy too. But only one name would make me truly happy. I held down the button until I reached the Lifemates section and found my name.

Andromeda Barliss matched to *Corvus Holmes*.

I stared at the backlit type, disbelieving. Had I read it wrong? I kept tracing my finger across the wallscreen, but every time it led me to the same name. Corvus was a perfectly fine boy, a little oafish, but he wasn't Sirius.

Scrolling down farther, I finally found *Sirius Smith* and connected the adjacent column: *Nova Williams*. My heart stopped—then it beat faster and faster until I feared it would burst out of my chest. I screamed, and Mom clicked off the food congealizer with a *zap*. I didn't wait for her to console me. I slammed my fist on the portal panel, stomped my foot while the particles dematerialized, and then ran into the corridor.

Tears blinded me as I pushed by people walking home from their jobs. I crashed into a service cart and toppled it over, sending tubes of liquid flying. The man behind it gave me an annoyed glare. "Watch where you're walking, missy!"

"Sorry, sir." I picked up a few of the tubes, replaced them on the cart, and stumbled forward. I had to find out what Sirius thought. I had to convince him to change the system.

There had to be a way.

When I reached his family's cell on the lower deck, I

pressed the portal panel and waited in agony until his dad paged me on the corridor's wallscreen. An older version of Sirius's face flashed on the pixels.

"Andromeda. Is there something wrong?"

Everything. My life, Paradise 21, the stupid Guide book. My entire world was wrong. "I need to speak with Sirius, please."

Silence. I wondered if he knew why I was there. Then his dad's voice came on again through the intercom. "I'll get him."

An eternity passed before the portal dematerialized. A few people gawked at me as they walked by. I must've looked crazy, hair pulled out of my braid and tears streaking my red-hot cheeks. Wiping at my face, I tried to compose myself.

Finally, Sirius emerged from the inner rooms. His face was set in serious lines and his arms were crossed. I wanted to part his arms and squeeze him, calling him mine.

He wasn't. He was Nova's. "Did you read the message?"

Sirius nodded, and his face clamped up. "I'm sorry, Annie."

"We can request a change—"

He shook his head and waved it off. He'd already come to terms with it, and his reaction infuriated me. How could he throw away what we had in a handful of milliseconds? "You know they don't honor requests."

I was falling, plummeting into a dark and scary black hole, and he wouldn't reach down to save me. "This wasn't how it was supposed to go."

"I thought it'd be different as well." He glanced down as if he couldn't stare into my eyes, black hair falling across his face in a shield. "I was stupid to believe we'd be together. Every question I answered correctly on that test brought me closer to the job I wanted, but I didn't realize it also took me further away from you."

My whole body trembled and I felt I'd fall into pieces

on his doorstep like a broken DNA model, beads tumbling everywhere. I stepped forward and moved to touch him, but he drew back into his family room. "I can't."

"Sirius, please."

"We can't continue this. Now that the assignments have been given, people will talk if we're seen together. There may be consequences."

"Since when have you cared about consequences?" I'd followed him on every adventure. He'd slanted the results of the test in his favor, and now he wanted to play by the rules?

Sirius kept shaking his head. "It will just hurt both of us."

As if I wasn't hurt enough? I grasped out and clutched thin air. Sirius disappeared into his family room and the portal rematerialized, shutting me out of his life.

One thought outweighed all the others: I should have kissed him when I had the chance. Maybe then, if he'd felt what it was like, he would have argued for both of us.

Staring at the portal in disbelief, I collapsed against the far wall, crumpling as though he'd blasted me in the stomach with a laser. My world fell apart around me as I realized how much he'd been a part of it. Now I'd lost him. He was gone.

Nova's words came back to me then in a thousand knives slicing open my heart. *Expects her grandpapa to just waste a high position on her.* She was right. My grandpapa would help me somehow manipulate the system to make it all right again. I hated asking him for a favor, but this was the one exception where I'd do anything.

Smearing my hand across my sniffling nose, I straightened up with new determination. Nova didn't deserve Sirius. I didn't care if they all thought I was spoiled; all I cared about was getting Sirius back. If it meant using my connections, then so be it. I stumbled over to the next hailing booth and punched in my grandpapa's frequency, waiting for him to answer.

Long moments passed and I wondered if he was busy with the operations of the ship to protect the lives of the entire crew, which was more important to everyone than my lifemate dilemma. A wave of guilt rose, but I pushed it back down as I stood waiting for his answer. His ghostly face stared at me, wires shooting from his flaky skin.

"Are we there yet?" I crinkled up my nose at my question. Why did I always say stupid things when I got nervous?

My grandpapa smiled faintly, humoring me. "Almost, Andromeda. I can see it on the horizon."

At least he wasn't confusing me with Great-grandma Tiff. He looked much more awake since our time in the emergency room. His calm composure gave me courage. "Do you have a moment to talk?"

"Of course. I always have time for you."

Relief poured through me. Maybe all I had to do was explain the situation to him and he'd set things right. "Good, because I have a favor to ask."

My grandpapa smiled bigger, his wrinkles creasing up in folds in his upper cheeks. "Anything you want, my dear. Come to the control deck and we'll work something out."

CHAPTER FIVE

PLEA

Bolting from the hailing station, I ran right into the one person on the entire ship I wanted to avoid.

"Corvus."

He stared at me with concern shining in his blue eyes. He wore his uniform tightly around his chest and the muscles protruded underneath. Other girls would giggle and blush, but he reminded me of an over-stuffed hero toy. "Andromeda, are you okay?"

"No. I mean, yes." I couldn't look at him. My eyes roamed everywhere else: a dent in the chrome wall, the metal grating underneath our feet. He reached out and put his hand on my shoulder, the same place Sirius had just a few days ago at the funeral. The gesture angered me. That was Sirius's spot.

I glared at him, and he blinked and removed his hand, scratching his short blond hair. Sirius's hair fell in beautiful waves across his forehead, tempting me to run my fingers through it, whereas Corvus chose the military buzz-cut. Simplicity appealed to him, and it irked me because so many shady areas lurked in my thoughts.

"You just look so…worried. Why are you running down the hall?"

I fumbled, trying to think what to tell him. The truth would be cruel. In all honesty, I ran from my pairing with him. "I have to talk to my grandpapa."

"Oh. Sorry to hold you up." He bowed his head down and stepped aside, leaving the hallway open for my passage through.

I didn't move. We paused, two statues frozen in awkward positions, and I studied him. Did he know about the assignments? If so, he gave no inkling. I wanted to snatch him up and lock him in a utility room until I sorted the assignments out.

But he was much bigger than me. I bet I could trick him into staying away from a screen. For all of his brute strength, he wasn't much of a thinker. That would take extra time, though, and I really wanted to get the assignments sorted out before he got his hopes up.

He looked so earnestly sorry about holding me up I decided to give him a few extra words. "That's all right." I moved past him, but his voice held me still. "Good luck, Andromeda."

The cheerful cadence in his tone didn't sound like him. I turned back, and he smiled.

"Thanks." I hurried to grandpapa, more confused than ever.

Guards stood at attention in two rows along the corridor to the control deck. Recognizing me, they parted and I wove a path in between them, trying not to look into their faces. I didn't want them to see the hurt etched in mine or the blasphemous question resting just beyond my lips. The portal to the control deck dematerialized and a current of cool, sterile air wafted out, blowing my hair behind me.

Grandpapa sat in the commander's chair, surrounded by tubes gurgling with clear liquid. Before him, the vast tapestry of space unwound beyond the main sight panel, reaching its way across the entire deck in a half-dome. In the center glimmered the pinprick of Paradise 21. I blinked and my breath caught in my throat. It seemed twice as big as before.

"Come in, dear Andromeda." He held up his hand and the tubes rustled, plastic crinkling. It pained me to see him in this fragile state, totally connected and dependent on the ship, but it was safer for him than wandering around in his hoverchair. The wires sprouting from his head seemed to hold him back so his head was tilted up. I could only see the bottoms of his eyes.

"What can I do for you?"

I fidgeted from foot to foot, trying not to look at the liquid flowing into his pasty arms. The scent of chemicals made my nose itch, but I ignored it and dared to go on. "We got our assignments today."

"I know. I assumed you'd be happy to work with your mom. You won't have to go far onto Paradise 21, and you can live beside the ship."

He knew me better than I knew myself. Yes, I'd be happy tending the newly planted turf fields with mom. What he didn't know was the shape of my heart.

"Yes, I'm fine with that."

He seemed to relax a little, slumping down to let the wires droop. "Good. Now what is wrong, my dear?"

I bit my lip. Could I really say it out loud? I thought of Sirius, and a hard edge formed inside me. As I spoke, my voice gained force until my last words rang clear and true against the glass behind us. "It's Corvus Holmes. I don't want him. I want to be paired with Sirius Smith."

The breathing apparatus connected to his neck rose and fell quicker, and a few tubes bubbled up with boiling water. Grandpapa's body tensed, and I feared he might have another heart attack. This time it would be because of me.

"Grandpapa!" I ran to him and threw myself into his lap, hugging his chest, willing him to be all right. "Are you okay?"

"Yes." His voice was faint, as if I heard him through

a fuzzy intercom. "I wasn't expecting that."

I pulled away and looked into his eyes, noticing they were the same pale blue as Corvus's and my own. "You can help me, right? You can change it?"

He shook his head, wires quivering. "I can, but I won't."

A fist squeezed in my chest, and my throat constricted. "Why not? You have the power."

He swallowed hard and paused. The familiar buzz of the engines filled the silence.

"You've been taught many times how the computer must assign mates to keep our small population from inbreeding, to keep our genes strong."

"We could look up Sirius's family history. I'm sure his ancestors were different from mine. The odds are—"

He shook his head as if it didn't matter. "I should have told you the real reason Aries Ryder ran away."

My thoughts ricocheted in my head. He'd changed the subject to something that had nothing to do with me. Or at least I thought it didn't. "What?"

"People say she didn't favor her job assignment, or the lifetime confinement on the ship drove her crazy. That's not the whole truth."

I didn't know what to say. The floor tipped underneath me and I swayed. "What is it, then?"

"She left the *New Dawn* because of me. I manipulated the system. I bribed the computer analysts and defied the assignments to make her my bride. I cheated, Andromeda. It was the biggest mistake of my entire life. Many people died because of it, and my actions threatened the entire course of this mission."

"That's not true. You were the one who found the mineral deposit on Sahara 354, providing enough energy for the ship to make it to Paradise 21. We wouldn't be here right now if it wasn't for you."

"A man named Smith found the mineral deposit, a distant ancestor of your friend Sirius." His gaze wandered above my head, as if looking back through time. "I was too consumed with anger and revenge to see it. Smith found it, but I reported it to the higher command."

"What does this have to do with me?"

"I'm not going to do it again, not for anyone. Tampering with the computer analytics is tempting the devil and opening Pandora's box at the same time. It will only put you in danger in the end."

"It brought you Great-grandma Tiff."

"Only after much pain and suffering. Trust me, I wouldn't give up Great-grandma Tiff for the world, but I must protect you from making the same mistake."

The control deck swam around me and I gulped down air as if drowning. There was resignation in his eyes. He wouldn't help me. I was doomed to be with Corvus.

"No."

"The quicker you accept it, the sooner you can move on with your life."

"No."

He cupped empty air with his old hands. "There is nothing more I can do for you."

I spat out my words. "Then there's nothing more I have to say to you."

I pulled away and scrambled to my feet toward the portal. As if he sensed my direction, the particles dematerialized immediately and the warmer air of the rest of the ship hit me like a hot bath.

"Forgive me, dear Andromeda."

His wispy voice followed me as I left him in his control seat to stew over his past and my predestined future. As I paced down the corridor with guards on each side, I felt as though I walked to my death.

CHAPTER SIX

ARRIVAL

"Attention. All colonists must be restrained in their containment cells by nineteen hundred. Attention—"

The calm woman's voice repeated in a looped recording and I covered my ears. They'd bleed if I heard it again. We'd spent the entire day securing every item we owned in large storage bins in the walls of our family's cell. I wondered if my antique glass snow globe from Old Earth would crack and wished I'd kept it out to hold in my hands.

Dad knocked his fist on a panel in the wall of our dining room and the metal retracted, exposing three seat carriers with various belts and buckles. I stared in awe at the place where the family portrait used to hang.

"These were built by the first astrophysicists as they fused together the chrome plates of the *New Dawn* six hundred fifty-eight years ago." Dad stared at them like they were some type of holy statues. They looked closer to a forgotten antique to me, old and cracked with worn plastic seats and tarnished buckles.

Beside me, my mom wrung her hands. "Let's hope they still work." She'd had to leave her precious biodome unattended. The Guide dictated that everyone onboard secure themselves in their cells during landing. With the entire population spread out, it would ensure the survival of the majority if one part of the ship were damaged during landing.

I hoped the greenhouses survived because the purple haze distorted the rays of Paradise 21's sun, and we had no idea how, or if, our food would grow in the ultraviolet light. I wasn't prepared to eat strange nectar and flower ovaries every meal.

"Everything will be fine, Delta." Dad gave Mom's arm a squeeze and turned back to flash a grin in my direction. "You heard the lady. Have a seat and strap yourself in."

Paradise 21 peeked out of the corner of the triangular window beside us, a glowing orb smothered with lavender clouds of cosmic dust. I stared, unable to tear my eyes away as I sat down.

"Secure your seat restraints, Andromeda." Mom's voice was shaky and high-pitched.

I huffed but said nothing. Would a leather strap really save me if the ship lost pressure, disintegrated upon entering the atmosphere, or crashed into the turf? Mom looked so nervous and scared I humored her, pulling it down across my chest and snapping the buckle into place by my thigh.

Panic fluttered my stomach. "What's happening?"

"Your grandpapa released the gravity rings." The string holding Dad's glasses around his neck floated up to his chin. "We don't need them anymore."

Silver arches floated by the window as the *New Dawn* shed its outer layers to enable landing. We could never fly in space again. That thought smacked me in the face, and my eyes teared up. We were stuck with whatever awaited us on Paradise 21.

Mom reached for my hand and squeezed. The rumble of the engines intensified as Grandpapa steered the ship into orbit. Mom's stew vibrated in my stomach, and I closed my eyes, hoping I wouldn't spew it up. I shouldn't have stuffed my mouth at dinner, but I always ate too much when my nerves acted up. To say I was nervous all day would be an understatement.

The ship pitched sideways and our dining room turned upside down. Bubbles of water from the faucet glided in the air around me like giant amoebas, and I held onto Mom's hand tightly.

"What's going on?"

"Grandpapa is figuring the landing coordinates." Dad craned his neck, looking out the window. "He needs to find a large body of water."

I broke out in goose bumps. What if the sight panel cracked when we landed and water came pouring in? I pictured it rushing through the window into our cell. Surely we'd get out in time, but even if we did, all our stuff would be ruined and we'd be forced to live as savages in the jungle of Paradise 21.

Suddenly I remembered the pair of scissors I'd used to cut the plastic wrap to preserve my uniforms. Did I remember to put them away? Try as I might, I had no memory of opening the storage bin. In fact, the last place I saw them was on the countertop in the kitchen. I scanned the adjacent room with wild eyes. A twinkle of silver caught my attention in the corner, the sharp blades spiraling around.

"The scissors! I didn't put them away!" I raised my hand as far as I could against my restraints and pointed to the far end of the room.

"Andromeda, how could you forget?" The harshness in Mom's voice punched me in my stomach. She put her hand on Dad's arm. "We can't have them floating around us as we land. They could take out one of our eyes."

"All right." Dad reached down and unbuckled himself. "I'll get them."

"No, Dad." I wiggled against my restraints and tried to hold him back but he'd already slipped out.

"Don't worry. I'll be fine."

He floated toward the kitchen, using the knobs on the

wall cabinets to pull him forward. The deep rumbling of the engines turned into a high screech and our family room shook as if we sat in a giant blender and someone had punched the *puree* button. We heard a thud from the kitchen. What if something hit him in the head? I screamed. It was my fault.

"Al! It's too late, come back!"

The ship pitched again and flipped us around so much I couldn't tell up from down. Dad's legs sprawled across the archway, and my heart beat so hard it hurt.

Mom dropped my hand and moved to undo her own restraints. I grabbed her hand and pulled it back. "It's too dangerous." What if they both died and left me completely alone?

Her eyes widened with fright. "I have to go get him."

She whipped her hand back and it slipped out of my grip. I struggled with my own restraints, but my shaky fingers couldn't unlock them. Just as Mom snapped out of hers, Dad appeared in the portal. Blood trickled from his head above his right ear. He spoke to us, but we couldn't hear him above the squeal of the engines.

Mom put her shoulder straps back on and extended her arms out, gesturing for him to come to her. He braced his legs against the wall and pushed, propelling himself toward us. Mom reached out and caught him as he floated by. "Al, you're hurt."

"It's okay. I just hit my head. It's not bad."

"Get back into your seat and I'll take a look at it."

Just as we secured him in his seat, the heat shields spread out around the ship in silver wings, blocking half the window, and the *New Dawn* tumbled through layers of atmosphere. Pressure crushed my chest and I struggled to suck in air, thinking each would be my last breath. The black, velvety space turned to a vibrant red-orange brightness.

The room rattled so much I feared my bones would turn to splinters and my body would be a glob of jelly with no spine. My teeth chattered and I bit into my tongue. The bitter, metallic taste of blood filled my mouth. A slate of metal careened by the window and I wondered if the ship was falling apart around us.

Parachutes whipped out like giant jellyfish, and the ship's descent slowed until I caught a glimpse of purple skies beyond the white nylon shifts.

I barely heard Mom's voice over the roar of the wind. "It's beautiful."

Dad squeezed my hand. "It's our new home."

I jerked in my seat as the *New Dawn* hit water. The window went from purple to a deep, dark blue, and bubbles raced up. I held my breath, but the glass didn't break. The water muted the engines. Had the landing ruined them?

I turned to Dad. "Will the engines work underwater?"

"Don't worry. After the momentum slows, we'll float back up to the surface." He'd wiped the blood from his face. His eyes were wide and alert. "Just wait."

He hadn't answered my question, and his omission made me nervous. As the ship slowed, shapes moved outside the glass—discs of white with numerous insect-like legs and ribbons of golden fish. I'd never seen another living being outside the *New Dawn*, and suddenly a vast bubble of life protected me. Deep space could no longer suck me out.

Just as Dad said, we began to rise, and the engines kicked in, steering us up. We broke the surface and bounced on the white-crested waves. I saw nothing but water and purple sky all around us.

The woman's voice came back on the intercom. "We have successfully landed on Paradise 21. Please stay in your seat restraints until further notice."

After what happened to Dad, I didn't question her. Sitting back in my seat, I breathed deeply to calm my racing heart and bubbly stomach, watching the waves swell against the glass.

"How long will it take?" I loosened the restraint across my chest to breathe easier.

Dad shrugged. "It depends on how far we landed from shore."

Although it was nighttime on the *New Dawn*, it was mid-afternoon on Paradise 21, and my eyelids drooped. I wondered if they'd have to change our clocks. The system was based off of Old Earth's sun, and we'd lost contact with the other colony ships hundreds of years ago, so it didn't matter anymore. Maybe they were reluctant to shed their last ties?

I drifted off to sleep, my head falling and bumping on my chest as the ship rose and fell with each squall. I don't know how long I was out, maybe two or three hours at most. The woman's voice woke me up, calm as ever.

"Attention. All colonists prepare for docking."

I rubbed my eyes and stared as a tangle of vines and monstrous flowers of impossibly brilliant colors claimed the coastline in a sprawl of dense jungle, tapering off onto a black sand shore.

My parents were already out of their seat restraints. Mom walked around the dining room, checking to see if our belongings survived the flight, and Dad packed a backpack with vials for soil samples, beacon lights, water bottles, and a video recorder.

"Are they planning to let us go out?" I unbuckled the snap at my thigh and shed the restraints, pulling them over my head.

"You bet." Dad winked at me. "But we shouldn't wander far."

"Mom, are you coming too?"

She slipped a laser knife in her shirt pocket and glared at me as if I questioned her reasoning. "It's for gathering specimens."

Before I could respond, the intercom buzzed again. "Docking successful. Report to the main auditorium for further instructions."

Before I could process the landing, Dad pressed the portal panel and the chrome dematerialized. "Come on, Annie, let's go."

Everything moved in a blur as we followed a stream of colonists through the main corridors to the front of the ship. We took our seats in the first pew of the congregation as always, but ahead of us lay a giant reminder that my world had changed forever. The vibrant colors of Paradise 21 cluttered the main sight panel in a thrashing wonderland, too strange to be true. All my life I'd stared out that sight panel and seen nothing but silky deep space, and now lush vegetation, sparkling waves, and a lavender sky cluttered the oblong piece of glass.

Grandpapa was slumped in his hoverchair, chest heaving. Tubes and wires trailed him like a bride's veil down the aisle as he floated to the main podium. Dried blood cracked around the input holes in his forehead where the wires rubbed against his skin.

This time he didn't disconnect from the ship, and I wondered if he was too weak to survive on his own for even a few minutes. His sacrifice pained my heart. But I didn't think of him as a saint. He was a flawed man with the same weaknesses I had, seeking his own path to redemption.

He'd asked me to forgive him and, in that moment, I did. I wanted to run to him and throw my arms around his neck. *Yeah, that would look really good in front of Nova and Sirius.*

Instead, I folded my hands in my lap and promised myself I'd get another chance to talk to him before he disappeared like Great-grandma Tiff.

When Grandpapa spoke, his voice was weak despite the amplification of his throat mic. "This is a momentous event in the history of mankind, a goal achieved throughout eight generations of steadfast work and perseverance. Because the space pirates severed communication with the other communal transport ships, we may be the last hope of humanity. Let us make our ancestors proud."

His arms rose feebly, but the surge of applause roared louder than anything I'd experienced in my life. Goose bumps prickled my neck as I pondered his words and watched the colonists around me celebrate their exhilaration.

Grandpapa gestured toward the emergency exit panel on the far side of the auditorium. "Preliminary atmospheric readings are compatible. Go now and take the first steps into a new future."

CHAPTER SEVEN

APPARITION

As the emergency portal dematerialized, a wash of humid air seeped in and I breathed in the heady scent of Paradise 21. The muggy tang of vegetation was heavy and sweet to the point of syrupy delirium. My nose tickled as if I'd stuck it right into the middle of a peach blossom and sniffed the pollen up to irritate my sinuses. I sneezed, then breathed again, trying to discern the complex fragrances mingling with the brine of the sea.

Dad led the way, stepping onto the plastic dock suspended three feet above the cresting waves. He gestured for me to follow, and I put a tentative foot on the platform. The grooves on the bottom of my space boots kept me from sliding. Mom followed behind. We were a trail of ants in a vast new place. *This world could swallow us whole.*

"Honey, make sure you hold onto the railing." The nervous edge to Mom's voice heightened my fears. Had I stumbled into a dream? I wished to wake up in the safety of my sleep pod, cocooned in the silence of space.

A shifting wind hit me, and the hairs on my bare arms rose with goose bumps. This world was all too real. I followed Dad, stepping above the deep, churning waters.

The wind increased, whipping my hair, and I pulled the wisps behind my ears only to have them blown in my face again. Clumps of foamy bubbles dotted the water, with spiraling vines thrusting up to clutch onto the platform. I stepped in the middle of the dock and prepared myself to kick any sort of vegetation away if it so much as brushed my leg.

"They're only seapods. They won't hurt you," Mom whispered to the back of my head as if she read my mind. The image of her slipping the knife in her pocket came back to me, and I wondered if she said it more to calm herself.

"I'm okay."

I jumped off the end of the dock and my feet sank into the black rock crystals. The gravity was stronger here than on the *New Dawn* and it pulled on my legs. My muscles screamed as I fought against it. The air was so full of oxygen it made me dizzy. My eyes watered, and the coastline smeared into a blotch of effervescence. Mom held my arm to steady me, but she wobbled too and we ended up clutching each other to stay standing.

The other colonists spoke in hushed tones as they spread out on the beach, their pristine white uniforms contrasting with the black sand and the emerald tangle of jungle hugging the coastline. Sirius jumped off the ramp and I broke away from my parents, heading toward him. The crowd blocked me, and Nova got there first, joining him at his side.

A fist squeezed my heart until it bled, and I froze in my stumbling tracks, gaping. Colonists walked by me, recording readings on their locators, and I thought I saw Sirius and Nova join hands in the glimpses I caught between the roving science team. When I looked again, they stood separately, Nova's hands resting on her curvy hips.

I resisted the urge to collapse in defeat on the black sand. Here I was on another world and all I thought about was being lovesick. Tearing my eyes away from them, I lurched toward the perimeter of the dense jungle. Bell-shaped flowers the size of my head drooped on large stems, shedding glittery spores on the black crystals of the beach. I crouched down and traced my fingertips along the glimmerdust, staining my skin with indigo and vermilion swirls.

"Beautiful, aren't they?"

I turned my head. Corvus towered over me.

I wanted to ask him what he was doing beside me, but I already knew the answer and it would seem rude. "I wish I remembered what they were called. I should have paid more attention in class."

"Yeah, me too." He smiled and crouched beside me, straining his eyes as if he tried to see what I saw in the black sand. Perhaps we'd failed equally miserably on the tests and that was why we were paired together. I gritted my teeth. Why had I been so lazy?

He touched the sand beside me, his large fingers clumsily brushing back the dark crystals and breaking the trails of glimmerdust in the sand.

I studied his broad forehead and wide-bridged nose, but his face gave no hint of emotion. He must've read the lifemate assignments by now, but if he had he didn't mention it.

I wanted to ask him what he thought about the whole pairing thing and how he felt about me, but my tongue stuck numb and heavy in my mouth. I could only crouch on the alien beach with him in awkward silence. What did it matter, anyway? I wasn't interested in him.

He reached out and his red-tinted fingers covered mine. He curled his fingers around my hand in the shade of the bell flowers. His hands were rough with calluses from constructing the Corsairs Sirius's deft hands would fly.

My fingers tensed and I shot him a sideways glance, arching my eyebrow. We stayed that way for a long time,

49

my question unanswered and his eyes watching me.

"Corvus, we need you." The older man's voice startled me, and I almost fell backward on my butt. Corvus had already removed his hand from mine.

"Yes, sir."

I whipped my head around, braid flying. A higher officer stood above us, impatiently shifting his eyes from our crouching position on the black beach to the ship. He pointed to a team of burly men unloaded monitoring equipment.

"See you later, Andromeda." Corvus bowed his head once and followed the officer to the ship, leaving me alone, teetering on the forest's edge. I looked down the beach. Mom scooped samples of the black sand into her vials, and Dad talked with other men. No one paid attention to me.

As my eyes returned to the tangle of flowers and vines, a glimmer of pure white light glowing deep in the jungle drew my attention. The sheen of light differed from the ruddy purple rays of Paradise 21's filtered sun, reminding me of the fluorescent lights inside the ship. I stepped from the beach onto the turf, the foamy membranes of interwoven plants.

The jungle floor squished under my boots, and I grabbed a vine the width of my hand to steady myself. Pin-sized insects with curling tails rose from the flowers around me and jittered off into the canopy of vines overhead. The heady scent of nectar intoxicated me, and I pulled up my uniform to cover my nose and mouth. Twirling stigmas and anthers splayed out of each blossom, reaching out to stain my white uniform with a rainbow of pollen. I remembered the bright hues of the man-eating giant we'd discussed in class, but I didn't see any flowers resembling it so I pressed on.

As much as I feared this new world, I didn't want to return to the ship and face my assignments. Both worlds collided and smashed me right in the middle. All I wanted was to get away.

The glow of light eluded me, drawing me farther into the jungle. The distant voices of the colonists faded into murmurs. I heard the buzz of tiny insects and the whisper of a faint breeze. The vines tangled around an outcropping of sharp stalagmites of crystal, gleaming like the inside of a geode in the purplish rays of the sun. A strange vibration shook the air, as if someone hit a tuning fork and let it ring. The light moved and I blinked, disbelieving. A gray silhouette emerged from the glow, and I fell backward into the flowers, the soft veiny petals brushing my skin.

The pollen released in my fall was so thick it obscured my vision, and I coughed, trying to clear my lungs and decide if I should run. The humanoid figure glided closer as if it floated above the turf. It had two bumps above each shoulder. At first I thought it was a backpack, but then I wondered if the lumps were folded wings.

Was it an angel? Had I died in the jungle? Been poisoned by some unidentified species or pulled into the stomach of a man-eating flower I couldn't even name? Trillium something. My mind whirled as the being moved toward me and came into focus. It wasn't an angel at all.

It was an alien.

I scrambled backward, but thorny vines clutched my feet. It stared at me through glassy pearls with no pupils, the eyes popping out of a slick opal-skinned face longer than it was wide. A beak-shaped nose below the eyes inhaled as it parted two plastic-looking lips.

I screamed and kicked until the vines bled a green, inky substance all over my white pants. Finally their hold loosened and I pulled myself up, sprinting through the dense vegetation. I didn't check to see where I tumbled as I threw myself forward. I could have stepped right into the Trillium what's-it-called monster flower's tentacles and died on the very first day.

A break in the vines up ahead gave me hope. I increased my pace, hearing the now-familiar sound of the waves rushing to the shore. I broke free of the jungle, plunging onto the beach into a whimpering heap. A few women collecting samples at the jungle's edge rushed to my side as I wheezed. A crowd gathered around me, everyone asking questions I couldn't answer.

Mom's voice cut through all of their gossip. "Annie, my goodness, what happened to you?"

She put her arm around me and I propped myself up on my palms, the crystal beach cutting into my skin. "I saw something in the jungle."

"Trillium Bisonate?" My mom pointed, and a couple of men with lasers ran in on the same path I came out on.

I gasped for air. "What?"

"The flower that eats people alive."

"No." I shook my head and swallowed. *Might as well come clean.* "An alien!"

Protests filled the air around me.

I stared at a member of the science team. "Check your life-form locator. Scan the surrounding perimeter ten meters into the jungle."

The man's fingers flicked over the keys. He shook his head. "Nothing…nothing but plants and insects."

Mom checked my forehead for a fever. "Are you sure you didn't mistake a flower? Or a shadow?"

Annoyed, I raised my voice. "It was humanoid. I'm sure of it."

Both men emerged from the jungle, shrugging and shaking their heads. Mom gave me a sympathetic look that only irritated me more. "You've had too many stimuli today. You need to rest." She turned to the nearest lifers. "Let's get her to the medical deck."

As they carried me to the ship, I checked the jungle line over my shoulder, expecting the alien to emerge and attack the colonists taking samples. Vines and blossoms stretched as far as my eye could see with no speck of otherworldly light. Maybe they were right. I did have pollen in my eyes, and all of the stress of the landing and seeing Sirius with

Nova may have caused me to hallucinate.

But even when I closed my eyes, the creature's pale face stared at me, beckoning.

CHAPTER EIGHT

SPECIMENS

I woke up in the same hospital bed Grandpapa had lain in. Sirius's face hung over me.

"Annie, are you okay?"

For a blissful moment I forgot about the alien, the tests, and the life assignments. Sirius and I were together again. I gazed into his silky brown eyes and lost myself.

"Annie?"

"I'm glad you're here." I reached up to brush his cheek with my index finger and he drew his face away, settling back in his seat beside my bed.

"I heard something happened in the jungle and I came to check on you."

It all came rushing back. Like it or not, my world had changed and there was no revisiting the past. I wanted to hide my head under my pillow and forget about it.

"They said you saw a creature."

The image of the pale alien face flashed in my memory and I winced. In the bright light of the emergency bay, the encounter seemed more and more hallucinatory. In any case, I wasn't ready to talk about it so I confronted him about something else. "How did you get into my room?

Only family can—"

Sirius put up a hand to silence me. "Annie, they all knew that we—"

"That we what?" Were friends? Were going to be matched up except for my stupid test scores? Although I knew a number of reasons, I still threw it back in his face with a glare.

His jaw tightened and he looked away. "Listen, I've got to go. I just had to make sure you were all right."

I wanted to grab his arm and make him stay, but I'd ruined the moment. There was nothing else to say. "Goodbye, Sirius."

He stormed off without another word, and guilt surged up because I'd sent him away.

Luckily, I had no time to dwell on it. The nurse came in and detached the tubes from my arms. She scanned a regenerator over the puncture holes and my flesh closed up with no scars. "Your father is here. You can go home."

"Great." I didn't sound very excited as I smoothed my fingers over the newly grown skin.

Dad waited by the portal to my medical cell. I cringed inside with embarrassment.

"Sorry, Dad."

His usually serious face broke into a small smile. "There's nothing to be sorry about. Your mom and I are just glad you're all right."

"I embarrassed you both."

He put a hand on my shoulder. "Nonsense. You've had too much going on, that's all. We all have, and it makes us see crazy things." He dismissed my apology as though he wanted the incident behind us as soon as possible, so I let my doubts go and followed him to our family unit on Deck Fourteen in silence.

As we entered the privacy of the elevator, he spoke in a hushed tone. "Listen, I know you saw your mom slip that laser knife in her pocket, but we're all safe here on Paradise 21. Scout satellites have explored the environment for years. Besides, after we brought you back to the ship, Grandpapa had teams comb the jungle around the shore. They looked for miles into the dense growth and found nothing."

Grandpapa involved several teams? Now I really *was* embarrassed. All of those people wasted their time because of me.

Dad must have seen my horrific expression. The elevator beeped and he pressed the door jam button, buying us time. "You have a lot to digest with the life assignments and the landing. You know you can talk to me about anything, right?"

"Sure, Dad." I squirmed under his attention. "But I don't need to talk. I'm fine."

The portal finally dematerialized and I took off into the hall. He wouldn't understand my situation. He loved Mom, and they were perfectly paired. Sometimes the stupid computers got it right.

Just as I assumed the day couldn't get worse, I turned the corner and Corvus sat in the hall next to my family's unit. He rose instantly, straightening his uniform across his large chest.

"Andromeda."

"Corvus."

Dad mumbled, fumbling with the panel to open the portal. "I'll let you guys talk, okay? Andromeda, I'll be in here if you need me. Dinner's in an hour."

I pleaded with my eyes. "Don't you need me to help?"

His eyes moved to Corvus, then back to me. "Mom's got it covered. You two have some catching up to do."

We were destined to be married, after all.

Corvus bowed as Dad entered our family unit. "Nice to see you, sir."

"You too, Corvus." With a swish of air the portal re-materialized, and Dad was gone.

This time I didn't think about being polite. I waltzed right up to Corvus and pointed my finger in the air. "What are you doing waiting outside my family unit?" *Just a little stalker-ish.*

Corvus shifted from one foot to another. I could tell he was nervous. "They wouldn't let me come into your medical cell since we're not, you know, not yet…"

My courage balled up inside me. "When did you find out?"

"Find out you were taken to the medical bay?"

"No." I wanted to roll my eyes. "Find out about us."

"Oh." His face turned as red as a dying sun. I wondered if he'd shrivel up and walk away, but he stood his ground and looked me straight in the eye. "The day the assignments were made. The message popped up on my computer, and I read it right away."

"Why didn't you say something to me when you saw me in the hallway?"

"I planned to, but when I caught you, you were in a hurry. Besides, I didn't know what to say."

I stood there gawking at him.

"I came today to see if you were all right. When I heard that something attacked you in the forest and you were taken to the medical bay, I wanted to come see you right away. I knew they wouldn't let me in, not being a family member…yet."

It would have been sweet had it not been Corvus. My tone softened a bit. "I wasn't attacked. I thought I saw something." I looked away, slightly embarrassed even though I really didn't care what he thought of me.

"Oh."

Corvus didn't press me. I guess he assumed it wasn't his place. Yet.

Instead, he started to ramble on about his experience. "There's some pretty weird stuff out there. I saw a few crazy things too." He took a hesitant step toward me and whispered, "After I moved all of that equipment, I went into the jungle in the place where you disappeared."

I leaned forward. Maybe he'd seen the same thing.

"And?"

"This vine wrapped itself around my leg. It just shot up from the ground and began winding. I took out my wire cutter and slashed it, but a part of it still clung to my leg. I had to pry it off."

"Wow." Although it wasn't as traumatizing as meeting an alien, I was surprised he'd shared his experience with me. I looked down at his leg. His uniform was torn, a big gouge taken out of it. "Are you okay?"

"Oh yeah, I'm fine. I was worried about you."

Although his eyes were a cold blue, his tone convinced me he felt something. A moment of weakness broke my composure. My encounter in the forest had built up inside me like an infection, and I had to tell someone. Maybe it would stop the image of the alien face from flashing in my mind.

"I thought I saw an alien, a humanoid." There, I'd said it out loud. I thought I'd be horrified that he knew, but instead it filled me with relief.

Corvus's eyes widened. "Really?"

I shrugged. "It was probably some hallucination from all the pollen, or from the stress of the landing and all this…change." I thought it wise *not* to mention seeing Sirius and Nova together.

"What if you did see something?"

"I don't know. Everyone I've talked to says I'm stressed. They think it was a hallucination."

"Listen, whatever it was you saw out there, I believe you. They want us to think they have everything under control; their super-successful satellites recorded everything there was to find on this planet before we even chose it to colonize. But what if they're wrong? What if there's something out there they missed?"

Corvus's words surprised me. I'd always thought he was Mr. Follow-the-Rules, the ideal military recruit, always obeying orders and performing his job with no questions asked. I didn't know he questioned stuff about Paradise 21.

I stood there like a wall hanging, not knowing what to say.

"Just be careful when you go out there and work on the crops with your mom, okay?"

I scratched the back of my neck, uncomfortable. If there were intelligent aliens living on Paradise 21 able to glide above the turf and fly, then none of us stood a chance. "I'll try."

Corvus leaned forward and my body tensed. Was he bending down to kiss me?

To my great relief, he reached in his pocket and brought out his wire cutter. "I want you to have this."

I took it, my hand brushing his. His thumb rubbed the back of my hand before I pulled away. Somehow, in the heat of the moment, I found his touch comforting. I ran my fingers over his initials engraved in the hilt. "This is yours. I can't. You'll need it for—"

"I have another one. Go on. It'll keep you safe."

I couldn't give it back, so I stuffed it into my shirt pocket. I was more likely to cut myself with it than harm any space aliens, but the weight pressing against my chest reassured me. "Thank you."

"Thank *you* for talking to me, Andromeda." It was almost as if he were saying *thank you for giving me a chance*. I wasn't sure I'd given him anything but false hope, but his gesture was sweet. I should give him something in return.

"Annie." I thought his nose didn't seem quite as big as I remembered. It was still nothing compared to Sirius's gorgeous face. "Call me Annie."

Corvus bowed his head like a knight from medieval Old Earth. "Whatever you like."

***

The next day I took Corvus's advice. As the first expedition teams left the *New Dawn*, Mom and I scouted the best place for the new greenhouses. She brought the laser knife and I brought along Corvus's wire cutter. We picked our way through the jungle, looking for a clearing, but the black crystal shoreline was the only place the vegetation refused to grow.

The vines rose over a ridge on the far left. At least it was different from the flatlands of the turf.

"What about over there?"

Mom checked her digital topograph. "It's a deep valley, formed by a crystal gorge."

I sighed, feeling boxed in by jungle on all sides. "Then where are we going to build our gardening facility?"

I wanted to suggest we go back and live on the *New Dawn*, but Mom wouldn't hear of it. Our mission was colonization, not vacationing. As much as I denied it, we were here to stay.

"I'll have to order a section of jungle cut down by a bio team." Mom charted the terrain with the topograph. "The jungle goes on for miles in every direction."

I peered up past the canopy of vines. Although it was early in the morning, the entire sky simmered into a faded purple, the same color as my nightshirt after it went through the cleaning cycle thirty times. Because of the clouds of cosmic dust surrounding Paradise 21, the sky would never be blue, and the sun never gold. The teachers had explained in science class how this particular sun was larger and stronger than Old Earth's, so we were lucky to have the extra protection. Still, I would have liked to have seen a gold sun in a blue sky.

As I followed Mom deeper into the jungle, I wondered about the other paradise planets. What was Paradise 20 like? Or Paradise 19? Maybe the *New Dawn* was stuck with the worst one. I stepped on a dead flower and it crunched under my feet, making me squirm.

"Why were we the ones given Paradise 21? Why couldn't we get a normal planet like Old Earth?"

"Honey, you know there's never going to be another Earth. Each paradise planet has its own advantages and disadvantages. We were lucky enough to get a planet with a perfect atmosphere and no humanoid indigenous species or other threatening predators. The colonists traveling to

Paradise 6 will have to deal with two years of darkness for every five years of light, and Paradise 12 is a low-oxygen environment so the colonists there have to wear space suits until their machines terraform the atmosphere. Compared to them, a purple sky and giant flowers don't seem so bad."

I laughed, surprising myself. "I guess you're right."

"Come on, you need to help me find this plant." She showed me a picture of a white flower on top of spindly sticks. "Its root system is supposedly connected to onion-like bulbs that might be edible. Let's take a few back to the *New Dawn* to study."

New species integration was, after all, my job assignment, and Mom had me get right to it. I pushed my way through a thicket where the vines used each other to clump together, forming pillars reaching up to the canopy. My legs ached and I thought of the alien, but I wanted to succeed at my new life assignment so I forced myself on.

An hour later, I stumbled upon speckles of white beneath a crystal outcropping. I lunged, my knees sinking in the turf, and plucked a small white flower. It had six round petals and a sprinkling of yellow in the center. This had to be it.

"Mom!" I reached down at the root system to yank it up. "I found it!"

Her boots crunched through the turf as she caught up with me. She broke through a veil of vines and stared, openmouthed. The tone of her voice was far from proud. "Andromeda, don't move."

"But I—"

I froze in mid-pull, stringy roots refusing to let go. She pulled out her communicator and typed a distress call.

"What is it?"

She cringed as though she couldn't decide if it would be worse to tell me or leave me hanging. Finally she pointed up above my head.

I craned my head with the slightest movement. A grove

of violet flowers as large as Landrovers were rooted on the crystal above. White tentacles drooped over my head like tongues, waiting to yank me in.

"Trillium Bisonate," Mom croaked. "They're provoked by movement. Don't run."

My whole body began to shake, and I remembered Corvus's wire cutter in my pocket. If one of them pulled me into its stomach, would I be able to cut my way out?

Her communicator beeped and she flicked her eyes down. "A bio team is on their way. Just stay put."

I held my breath until I feared my lungs would burst and then exhaled slowly, trying not to rustle the vines surrounding me. A white tentacle moved aimlessly, reminding me of an arm twitching while someone slept. It dangled a foot above my head, and I contemplated how much movement it would take to reach in my pocket and slash it with the wire cutter.

Mom's face curled up in agony as she watched, helpless. "I shouldn't have let you go out so far on your own."

"Mom, I'm seventeen, not nine," I whispered in a hiss. "It's my fault. I wasn't watching the sky."

She bent down and grabbed a sharp shard of crystal, and I widened my eyes in warning. "Don't do it, Mom. Don't come over here."

"If it moves, I'll throw this to the left and you run to the right, okay?"

"Sure." My voice didn't sound so certain. Above me, the tentacles moved listlessly in the breeze. There were tiny suction cups on the tips, and I shuddered at the thought of the membranes sticking to my skin. A drop of nectar fell on my shoulder and a tiny insect landed next to it. The multi-legged bug crawled toward the drop and extended a long black tongue, sucking up the nectar.

I clenched my teeth and resisted the urge to swipe it away. Goose bumps prickled the back of my neck, and I thought this moment would last forever: Mom gawking, me crouching, and the insect feasting.

Stray wisps of my hair blew in the breeze, coming dangerously close to the end of a tentacle. A blond strand brushed the suction cup, and it stuck to the wet membrane. My instinct told me to jerk my head away, but I stayed put.

A blur of movement caught my attention from the edge of my sight. Laser blasts erupted over my head. My mom screamed, "Annie, move! Now!"

I scurried away as the sky rained petals. Mom reached out and pulled me behind the bio team. They fired until the violet flowers were nothing but mush and an ugly hole penetrated the canopy of vines. Although the flowers could have killed me, guilt trickled through me as I stared at the remains. It seemed wrong to trespass and destroy everything in our path. We were just as bad as Christopher Columbus.

"They'll make sure that species grows nowhere near here, okay, honey?" Mom gripped me as if I'd come back from the grave. Although she meant it to be reassuring, the vengeful thought stirred up a strange mix of love for Mom for wanting to keep me safe and remorse for the planet that had no idea we planned to conquer it.

CHAPTER NINE

POISON

I watched from the triangular sight panel in the dining room as Landrovers tore down the part of the jungle Mom had ordered the bio team to clear. After an initial wave of destruction, a foot-crew yanked up the turf, disentangling the roots of a massive network of vines, revealing black crystal underneath. They stripped the land until it looked bare and naked, like a giant had chomped down and bit off a colossal chunk. Once the bio team cleared the designated area, construction crews put up the smoky glass of the colony's new greenhouses, in rows.

Mom twiddled her fingers by the sight panel, impatient to expand her crops. She'd already introduced the black crystals to the soil in the biodome and had enormously successful results. Although we'd learned Earth plants withered underneath the naked purple rays of this planet's sun, the smoky glass of the greenhouses would filter the blazing ultraviolet light.

"Go on, Annie. Try it."

A ripened tomato, twice as big as my palm and plump as a baby's bottom, lay on the countertop. My mouth watered just looking at the shiny red sheen. Yet, because it was grown with the new crystals, I was hesitant to sink my teeth in.

"If it took millions of years for the crystals of Paradise 21 to form, don't you feel bad grinding hundreds of them into dust to enrich Old Earth's soil?"

"Oh, Annie." Mom squeezed my arm as we looked out to the newly forming greenhouses. "It would take thousands of years to use them all up." She gave me her practical look—half smile and half frown. "We must consider our immediate needs first. There's an entire colony going hungry."

"What will our descendants do when the crystals run out? Find another planet and strip it bare? Or worse, poison it like they did Old Earth?"

"That's something for the later generations to consider hundreds of years from now. Right now we have to worry about ourselves. You of all people should know our soil has turned barren after eight hundred years of excessive use, and now I can use the crystals to infuse nutrients into our crops. You've seen how high the nitrogen is in just one ounce."

I had. It was amazing. The black crystals provided excellent fertilization, but it was the purple crystals that, when ground up and sprinkled over the soil, achieved accelerated growth. I'd been charting the crops' progress now for a week, and the results had surpassed every hope we'd ever had. I should have been elated, but a sharp pang of remorse held me in check.

Before I could debate any further, a message beeped on the main wallscreen in the living room. Mom jumped up. "My goodness, it's your great-grandfather."

She sprinted over to the panel and pressed the video button. His face flashed on, large as the living room wall, and for a second I imagined him as the giant biting off a piece of Paradise 21.

"Delta, we need you in the emergency bay. It's urgent."

Mom leaned in until her body covered his entire nose.

"Is everything okay?"

"A member of the bio team has fallen ill. I need you to analyze the composition of the toxin and deduce whether it came from any infectious agents on Paradise 21."

"Okay. I'll go immediately."

"Good. He's in patient cell 43-F. We need this species identified at every stage of its life so we can eradicate any further contamination. If it's lethal, you must work with the other scientists on a cure."

"Yes, Commander." Although he was Mom's grandfather-in-law, she always called him by his formal name. Mom moved to shut off the screen, but my grandpapa's voice held her still.

"And Delta—"

"Yes?"

His voice grew tender. "Be careful. Take care of Andromeda."

I guess he hadn't noticed me sitting in the background. His concern for me outweighed any grievance I had with his diplomatic policies. I was touched. I still hadn't told him I accepted his apology, and it reminded me I needed to take time and visit him on the obsolete main control deck.

"I will." She shut the screen off. "Come on, Annie, let's go."

"I'm going, too?"

"You're part of my team now, and I'll need someone to double-check my readings."

I didn't know whether to feel proud or scared. Yes, she trusted me with this extremely precarious situation, but could I really do anything to help? My low test scores haunted me, furthering my self-doubt, and I had to push them away.

"All right." I picked up my backpack, although I couldn't think of anything inside that would help me. "I'm ready to go."

We hurried down the corridor and pressed the elevator panel to take us up to the medical emergency bay. I thought of the poor contaminated man and wondered if he was conscious or if he was in pain. Corvus was right. They hadn't prepared for everything. The satellites had never picked up a potentially poisonous contaminant. If they were wrong about that, then they could be wrong about a lot of things.

The alien's pale face surfaced in my mind, and I shook my head to remove the image, as if the thought would summon the creature beside me.

The portal dematerialized, and we rushed down to cell 43-F. Guards stood by the entrance, holding off a swarming crowd of colonists asking questions and demanding answers. They handed us each a face mask before allowing us to go in. I snapped mine around my head, the elastic pulling at my hair, and followed Mom into a room full of nurses and scientists. She forced her way to the bedside and pulled me with her.

Ray Simmons from the class one year ahead of mine lay in the bed. A jolt of panic shot through my veins. It could have been me lying there. Sweat covered his face, and his eyes flickered around blindly as if he was having a seizure.

Mom whipped out her hand-held digital pad to take notes. "Did he mention any unusual plants?"

An older man who looked vaguely familiar to me, perhaps a supervisor, walked over to her. "He hasn't spoken since we found him face-down in the jungle turf."

"Did you collect a sample?"

His eyes were hard coals. "No. I evacuated the area immediately. I'd like you to slip on a full-body suit and head a bio team with me to retrieve what we can."

I'd never seen Mom's eyes stretch that wide. "I'm a microbiologist, not an explorer."

He gave her a no-nonsense grimace. "Exactly why you're the one we need. You'll know what to look for."

Mom shook her head violently. "I have no idea what to look for. The satellites didn't report any poisonous plants. There's no evidence of anything on this planet that can harm us besides the Trillium Bisonate."

"We need your expertise."
Mom's voice grew low. "My job is to take care of the crops."

Disobedience was not in this man's vocabulary. "You have a new job now. Assemble your bio team. We'll be heading out at dawn tomorrow."

As the adults argued behind me, I pressed my way forward to Ray's bedside. I grabbed his hand, wrapping my fingers around his cool, damp palm. As I squeezed his hand, his gaze focused on mine and became lucid. I stared into the eyes of a drowning man, fearing what I might see. I wanted to save him, but I had no way to research a cure until I knew what he suffered from.

"What did it look like, Ray?"

He stared at me blankly.

"Ray, what did this to you? What did you see?"

When he spoke it was barely a whisper. "They tried to warn me, but I didn't listen."

His words made me shiver.

"Who?" I leaned in closer and wisps of my hair fell onto his chest.

He shook his head as if I wouldn't understand, and the machine connected to him started to beep faster. I had a feeling we didn't have much time to get through to him.

"What did you see?"

"Goes…." He was so weak he could barely breathe, never mind speak, but I had to try.

"What? Goes?"

He took a sharp intake of breath. "Ghos…" His voice died before he could finish the first word. The pulse of his heart increased and his body went rigid as a board.

"Ray, stay with me." I held onto his gaze, pleading with him to keep his eyes focused.

He squeezed my hand so hard I feared my fingers would pop out of their joints. Behind us, the heart monitor went berserk.

I slammed my elbow against the code button on his bedside and an alarm beeped, silencing the argument behind me. "Something's wrong."

Nurses rushed to his side, covering his mouth with a mask attached to a ventilator, and Mom pulled me to her as if I was too young to take it, as if she could shield me from the horrors of this new world.

I pulled free. I didn't want to sit snug in my cocoon any longer. Whether I liked it or not, we were stuck here on this strange jungle planet. I had to play the cards I was dealt. I wanted to find out who the alien people were and what did this to poor Ray.

"I'm coming with you." I yanked my hand away from hers as Ray struggled to breathe. Behind us, the nurses stabilized his condition by injecting him with a sedative.

"You can't, Annie. You've got no experience on this new world."

I jutted my jaw out and challenged her. "Neither do you."

CHAPTER TEN

RECONNAISSANCE

"Stay behind me and don't take off your bio-suit." Mom shoved plastic vials for samples into her backpack. Her anger with me and my big mouth had simmered to a slow boil, and after a few hours of pestering she put my name on the bio team list. "Keep your eyes open. We don't want another incident."

I looked away, ashamed. An image of torn petals raining on the turf seared my memory. "I said I was sorry."

"But you didn't say you'd be more careful."

"I will." I tightened the straps around my waist, but the bio-suit still flounced around me like a marshmallow, as if my shirt and pants were stuffed with clouds. Good thing no one but the other members of the bio team would see me in such a pouffy state.

Mom's bio-suit fit her just right. She pulled the plastic hood over her head and sealed the sides around her neck in the practiced way of a true explorer. "Promise me you'll pay more attention to your surroundings."

"I promise." I wasn't five years old, following her through the bio dome on a routine inspection. She never used to let me handle the plants, slapping my roving fingers until I kept them by my sides.

"Don't touch anything with your bare hands. Put as many samples as you can in the vials."

"I know." I seethed with exasperation.

She gave me a warning glance and I bit my tongue to hide my sour attitude. She'd use anything to get me to stay home. I swallowed my pride. "Thank you for taking me along."

"Well, you were right to ask to go. As a new member of the bio team, you should do anything in your power to discover more about your environment. You need to learn about this planet just as much as I do, or more if you want to progress up the ranks." She softened her tone. "As my daughter, I'd rather you stay where it's safe."

It was the closest I'd get to Mom getting sappy on me, and I kind of liked it. I smiled, but she stuffed extra sample vials in her backpack, unaware. "Come on, the Corsair leaves in an hour and I want to be on time."

No one was there to bid us goodbye. Dad had left several hours ago. Since they didn't need him to monitor the ship's engines, Grandpapa reassigned him to a research team. Now he researched the best way to power our new colony off the ship. He rose every day at dawn and didn't come home until hours after the purple sun set each night.

As I looked behind me at the empty family room, wistfulness clouded my thoughts. I missed our lives before the landing. Both parents came home and made dinner, and we ate together around the table. There were no dangerous missions, no dire contaminants.

I sniffed up my self-pity. My life was different now, and the sooner I coped with that the better I'd do. Picking up my backpack, I followed Mom out the portal.

The loading dock bustled with commotion. A team of Landrovers filed out on a ramp, destined to flatten another stretch of land for housing units, and exploration Corsairs took off every fifteen minutes into the deep violet sky. Mom directed me around the hustling colonists to a smaller torpedo-shaped ship toward the rear.

I recognized the man in charge of the mission from the emergency room. He came forward and shook Mom's hand. "I'm glad to see you're ready."

"As ready as I can be, Lieutenant Crophaven."

Lieutenant! My eyebrows rose. There were only three lieutenant positions on board the ship, so he outranked Mom and Dad by several levels. I wondered why I hadn't noticed who the lieutenants were before and scolded myself for being so self-absorbed.

If you wanted anything done, the lieutenants were the people to ask. Grandpapa had risen to the revered position through many years of hard work, and from there the previous commander appointed him as his replacement. No wonder Mom lost the argument in the emergency bay.

"Let's go over the routine procedures." Lieutenant Crophaven pulled out an old clipboard with real paper on it, and I leaned forward to get a good look.

Mom turned to me. "Go on, Annie. Belt yourself in."

"Okay." I knew when I wasn't invited. Letting her discuss the particulars with the lieutenant, I approached the Corsair, wondering if the motion of flying would make me sick. I'd flown my entire life on the New Dawn, but this ship was much smaller and navigated air currents, not deep space. As I stepped up the narrow metal staircase to board, a familiar face was at the control panels, and my heart squeezed so hard blood trickled in my chest. I wanted to shrink back down before he saw me in all my pouffy glory, but it was too late.

"Andromeda."

"Hey, Sirius."

"I didn't think you'd be coming on this mission."

Ouch. The muscles in my chin quivered. Just because I tested low didn't mean I wasn't involved in important things.

"I didn't know you'd be flying us into it."

"I won't." He looked away. "I'm the first officer. Lieutenant Crophaven will be flying today. I'm training for the next set of missions."

"Oh." Somewhat placated, I smoothed down the front of my bio-suit, but it popped right back into place. Embarrassed and angry, I wiggled my way past the cockpit. "I need to belt myself in."

"Annie." He grabbed my arm and tugged me toward him. My heart tugged as well. "Be careful today. I heard this mission is particularly dangerous. There's already one man down."

"I know. I saw him." My voice came out more edgy than I would have liked, and I tried to soften it. "I'll be fine."

"Passengers, take your seats." The lieutenant's voice boomed behind us as he leapt up two stairs at a time. "Miss?" He gestured for me to move, and I looked down at Sirius but he'd already let go of my arm.

"Of course." I felt like a fool standing in the way and scurried to the farthest seat in the rear of the Corsair. Mom joined me, and we belted ourselves in. Two of Mom's coworkers and a third woman wearing a medic's coat settled in the seats in front of us. I recognized two of them from my trips to the biodome and tried to manage a friendly smile as the engines revved up. Nerves bubbled up in my stomach, and I resisted the urge to bite my nails. My hands and arms tingled as the ship pushed off the ground and hovered.

The deck swayed and my stomach heaved. The engines grew louder, rumbling my bones and buzzing in my ears. Mom said something, maybe trying to comfort me, but I couldn't hear her over the clamor. I closed my eyes and willed myself not to throw up as we sped forward, vaulting into the open sky.

The vines below me were an intricate tapestry sprinkled with pieces of purple and ebony shards. The aerial view of the terrain inspired awe, and I couldn't imagine flattening it for greenhouses and housing units, but that's what we did each day, balding a patch of jungle with our relentless machines.

We flew farther than I expected, coming up just beneath the crystal mountain ridge.

Mom leaned in. "We're headed down."

She took my hand, and I squeezed her hand as the ship dropped, my heart and stomach plunging with it. Gripping the arm rest of the chair with my other hand, I swallowed, trying to keep my breakfast down. We're descending too fast. The jungle canopy rushed up, and I thought for sure we'd crash. Reverse thrusters engaged, and the ship slowed. We hovered just above the reach of the vines.

The aviator's voice came on the intercom. "We've arrived at the specimen site. You are now free to move about the bay."

Sirius rounded the corner and opened the hatch, dropping out a coil of rope ladder.

I turned to Mom. "We're going down using that?"

She gave me an apologetic smile. "I forgot to tell you. The Corsair can't land here. We have to climb down."

"Great," I muttered under my breath. This mission just gets better and better.

"Put on your filter mask." Mom's voice sounded muffled as she tightened her own. "We don't know what the plant looks like, and it could be anywhere in this vicinity."

I adjusted the elastic straps until the plastic sucked my face off, and inhaled my first breath of filtered air. "Okay."

"Good."

I followed the rest of the bio team as they collected their gear and filed in a line by the portal. One by one, they started down the ladder. I was the last one to leave the ship. As I turned back to the cockpit to position myself over the rope ladder, Sirius put his hand on my shoulder and spoke over the roar of wind bolstering the ship's belly. "Good luck, Annie."

I stifled a rising thread of hope that he still cared for me and tried to keep my face even. "Thank you." I wasn't sure he heard my muffled voice through the filter.

"Be careful." His eyes sparkled with intensity, and I wondered what else lurked in the depths. Did he look at everyone that way? Or was his fiery gaze meant only for me?

Lieutenant Crophaven muttered a question behind him and Sirius disappeared into the cockpit. I stepped down to the fourth rung of the ladder. The violent wind of the hovering Corsair ripped through me, almost blowing me off-kilter. I tightened my grip on the top rung, trying not to look at the rush of green beneath me. One hand over another, I climbed down in my pouffy bio-suit.

When I got to the bottom, I jumped the remaining distance and landed on my hands and feet in a crouching stance in the turf. The foamy latticework of roots and vines had cushioned my fall. I recovered quickly, rising to meet the group.

Mom tapped a pair of tweezers against her palm. "Let's start taking samples."

I followed them into the jungle, stopping along the way to pluck offshoots of plants I didn't recognize and drop them into plastic vials. The samples rattled around in my backpack with each step. I wondered if any of them would lead us to an answer, or if we were all on a wild comet chase.

The group fanned out over the landscape, combing the jungle. I stayed within earshot of Mom, making sure to use the ridge as a reference point. Determination hardened inside me. I wanted to be the one to find the culprit releasing the toxin. I'd disappointed her so far, and today I longed to make her proud.

Compared to the buzzing engines of the Corsair, the jungle lay silent with only the occasional drip of rain trickling off the vines. I climbed my way through a tangle of creeping plants and found a conglomeration of hand-sized white flowers under an outcropping of purple crystals. Spiral stigmas dusted with corn-colored pollen jutted out of the center of the petals.

Securing my mask, I reached down and swiped a cotton swab against the blossom until enough of the yellow pollen stained the tip. Popping open a vial, I dropped the swab in just as a flash of movement beside me caught my attention.

I froze, turning my head slowly so as not to draw attention to myself, and spotted a glow of white light just beyond a thicket of ferns.

The same glow I'd seen on the first day.

My whole body tensed up. My fingers darted to my locator, but for some reason the screen wasn't working. Should I go back and alert the team, or go after it? The light diminished as I crouched in indecision, and I jolted upright, cursing. Instinct kicked in, and I pushed forward through the vines. The light lured me forward, always teasing me behind clusters of ferns and large blossoms. I tripped and fell, and my face jammed into the vines. Pin-sized insects fluttered around my face. I glanced up feverishly, thinking I'd lost it. The glow hovered just beyond a column of vines.

Pulling myself up, I followed it until the vines ran together in a blur. The crystal mountains towered over me like giants condemning my trespassing. The jungle darkened in their shadow, making it easier for me to spot the light. I broke free of the vines and crested a ridge, climbing on slabs of sheer crystal. My breath heaved in my ears and plumed against the inside of my mask. Behind me lay the jungle and in front of me jutted the foothills of the mountains. I'd traveled far from our assigned range.

The white glow solidified into a humanoid shape and I held my breath, waiting for it to make a move. It was too far away to be threatening, so I stood my ground, wishing my locator still worked.

I could make out the shape of the wings and the piercing stare of its round eyes. Its arm rose, the wing attached to it fanning out in a blur of iridescence. It extended a long branch-like finger toward the mountainside. I crept forward on the rise of crystal, trying to see what it was pointing at.

The slant was steep, and my feet slipped forward. I scrambled for a handhold, my arms flailing as I tried to keep my balance. A stray piece of crystal rolled under my boot and I skidded, tumbling head over heels until I hit the turf. Pain shot up my leg and I looked down to see my foot bent at an odd angle. I hit my fist into the turf, breaking stems. "Damn it."

The panic rose in a tidal wave. I breathed hard, trying to talk myself out of hysteria. Calm down. Try to get up.

I counted to three and rose. A streak of pain overwhelmed me and I cried out, settling back on the ground. Now I'd done it. I'd broken my leg. Mom would never let me come on another mission again.

Panic rose up, constricting my throat, as I realized I couldn't make my locator work and I was stranded. Would I die of thirst and hunger out in the jungle?

Calm down. You couldn't have wandered too far from the team. They certainly won't leave without you.

The muscles in my arms bunched and burned as I dragged myself into the foliage and away from the ridge. Sharp pains stabbed my ankle every time my leg bumped against a vine. Tears blurred my eyes, and I thought of all the people who I'd let down.

I have to get back. I needed another chance to find this toxin, and to prove to Mom I was the best species integration assistant she could ever have. I refused be labeled a slacker for the rest of my life.

Gritting my teeth, I fought through the pain and climbed over the weave-work of vines. My bad foot kept getting tangled and I had to tear my boot free, eliciting more sharp pains and more tears. The sunlight began to fade, and a new rush of adrenaline surged through me as I realized I'd be alone in the dark of night. No one had built energy panels into the crystals. I couldn't just reach up and bring light with the touch of a finger. Man, was I spoiled on the New Dawn. I'd never look at my sleep pod the same way.

Just as another wave of frustration came over me, my locator beeped and the screen flashed back on. I hailed Mom's locator immediately, typing the distress code followed by a burst of my assigned signal so she could find me. She responded immediately with a beep and a single line. Coming to get you.

Relief intoxicated me and I collapsed with my face in the vines. What would I tell her? I followed a wandering white light and climbed up a sharp and dangerous crystal for a better look? Was I going crazy?

Mom broke through the jungle along with the medic from the bio team.

"Andromeda! Thank goodness we found you."

A new wave of embarrassment hit as Mom rushed over. The medic, an older woman with white hair and wrinkles spreading from her eyes, knelt beside me, feeling around my foot and leg. At least her fingers were gentle.

"It's sprained. Nothing more." After wrapping my ankle in a tight brace, the medic packed up her supplies.

Mom gave me a warning stare. "You're lucky. You could have snapped your leg in half. What were you doing out here?"

"Research." I shrugged. "At least I thought I was."

Thank goodness the medic interrupted. "Help me hoist

her up." Mom sighed and propped me up against her while the medic took the other side. Being dragged was humiliating, but the pain was too much to bear just for my pride.

After an arduous trek back in silence, we reached the hovering Corsair. Lieutenant Crophaven scowled as he attached me to the ladder. Did the man ever smile? Looking at the frown lines in his tight-lipped face, I didn't think so.

Sirius pulled me up so I didn't have to climb.

As I reached the landing, Sirius grabbed my arm and hauled me up onto the floor of the Corsair. I thought I'd die of embarrassment, but I wasn't so lucky. I had to stay there with him alone until the rest of the bio team finished their scan.

"Annie, what happened? Are you all right?"

I didn't want to tell him I saw another crazy alien no one else saw, again. So I shrugged, trying not to make it such a big deal, although it was. "I slipped on a crystal and fell."

"Does it hurt?" He helped me onto my seat and propped up my foot.

"Not very much." Actually, my whole leg throbbed as though it had been ripped off, but I wasn't going to act like a baby. Not after being such a foolish klutz.

"Let me hold a cold bar on it."

"That's okay. You don't have to." Sirius had already opened a container and retrieved a plastic stick, which he bent in half to activate the chemicals. He sat beside me and applied a bit of pressure to my ankle with the cold bar. It felt worlds better as it numbed. I wished I could numb myself, because my heart beat fifty times too fast.

Sirius had a distant look in his eyes. "Annie, remember when we broke into the biodome at night and let all the goats free?"

Despite the situation, I laughed. "Yeah. One of the

nanny goats bit that old desert cow from Sahara 354 and it snorted water out from its third trunk."

"Or was it the fourth?" Sirius punched me gently in the arm.

"You never did tell your mom how your uniform got so dirty, did you?"

He smiled slyly. "Nope."

He was trying to get my mind off the pain. It worked like a miracle. Why did he have to be so charming?

Something must have changed in my eyes because Sirius stopped smiling and his voice grew soft. "What's wrong?"

I sighed, debating whether or not to tell him anything. My impulsiveness won. "We can't have adventures anymore."

Sirius spread his arms. "Look at us, Annie! We do have adventures. Now they're far better. Now they're real."

"Ha." A bitter chuckle rose in the back of my throat. "Real." What we had before was more real to me than what we had now. How could I tell him that? Did I want to?

He shrank into himself like a cornered animal. "Annie, I'm just trying to do my job. You have to have faith in the path the Guide chose for us. If you can't believe that, then how can you believe in anything we do here?"

"I believed in us," I blurted out.

I'd never openly mentioned our "couple" status out loud. Sirius started as if I'd electrocuted him back to life. His gaze intensified, and he bent his head next to mine. His breath teased my lips. The temperature in the ship seemed to rise to a hundred degrees.

We teetered on the verge of another kiss. This time he pulled away. "I hear them coming."

At first I thought he'd made up an excuse, but then the rope ladder twitched with movement. Sirius cast me one last longing look and went to help the bio team board the ship. I settled back in my seat with my numb foot resting on the back of the chair in front of me and wondered why the world had to be so many shades of purple and not just black and white.

CHAPTER ELEVEN

MASKS

Mom exiled me to one of the outer greenhouses beside the *New Dawn*. None of the samples from our mission came back positive, not even mine, so all we had to show for our efforts was my sprained ankle. Failure overwhelmed me until I felt as though I sat at the bottom of a giant recycling chute with no way to ever climb out.

As I pruned gi-normous tomato plants reaching far above my head, I watched through the smoky glass of the greenhouse as workers constructed a central town square. Landrovers, cranes, and work crews trampled over what had once been quiet, untamed jungle. Judging from the size of the foundation of the latest building, it would be a skyscraper resembling the ones in the cities back on Old Earth. A part of me grew excited at the prospect of having anything resembling something from Old Earth, but another part of me knew we'd stolen this planet.

The outer portal opened with a whiff of humid air and Mom barged in. I straightened as much as I could on my shoulder crutch and pretended to be working hard. The irrigation ditches needed to be dug, and I still hadn't watered the plants.

She had to pull down her filter mask to speak clearly. After Ray's sickness, we were all supposed to wear them outside the *New Dawn*. "Wait until you see what I've found!"

At least she was in a good mood.

I watched openmouthed as men dragged in a large outcropping of deep violet crystal shards on a dolly, wheels screeching under the weight. The sight of the crystals made me uneasy and I shrank back. Every time I stood around them, I saw those strange aliens.

"Why do you have to bring it in here?" Would they attack us for taking so much of it? I certainly hoped not, considering no one except for me believed in their existence, and I'd be the one to work near the stolen crystal, *alone, every day*.

"It will be easier to grind the crystal here, where we can instantly add it to the plant soil." Mom surveyed the team. "Put it over there, by the cucumbers."

"Yes, ma'am," a bass voice answered her.

I turned quickly, recognizing the voice. "Corvus?"

He pulled down his bio mask, a hint of a smile on his lips. "Hi, Annie."

I wondered if his superior ordered him to drag it in or if he took the job knowing I'd be there.

Either way, there he was.

I watched the broad muscles in his shoulders tense up as he handled the brunt of the heavy lifting, placing the chunk of crystal shards in the corner of the greenhouse where it refracted rays of purple sunlight like a rainbow-maker.

Clapping his gloved hands together to shed the purple dust, he nodded in Mom's direction. "Just as you wanted it, ma'am."

"Thank you, Corvus. Isn't that what Andromeda called you?"

"Yes, ma'am."

"Corvus Holmes?"

His blue eyes sparkled with amusement. "That's right."

Mom's eyes darted back and forth between me and him, putting pieces of a larger puzzle together. She offered him her hand. "Nice to meet you. We should have met much sooner, and I apologize. I've been very busy with the greenhouses."

"No worries, ma'am." Corvus took her hand and shook it gently.

She smiled a little too big, and my cheeks burned. "I'll leave you two alone, then. Annie, get to the watering before the sun dries out our best crop yet."

"Yes, Mom."

With a wink in my direction, she led the other men out of the greenhouse and left me there with Corvus and a whole lot of awkward tension.

"How's your leg? I heard you sprained your ankle."

I looked into his cool blue eyes and searched for something more. Could he make me feel the way Sirius did? Sirius had tempting warmth in his dark eyes and Corvus's light blue ones were calm and cold as jewels. "It's not too bad. I can still get around."

"Good." He picked up a fallen leaf and twirled it between his thumb and forefinger. "Listen, they're having a celebration tonight: a light show with dancing and techno music."

I'd heard about it but I wasn't planning on going. My ankle throbbed, and I still had a lot of work left to do from procrastinating all day. "Yeah, I know."

"Do you want to go with me? I heard they'll let us take off our masks."

I shifted my weight to relieve the soreness under my arm. "No masks?"

"Yeah, they said the air's safe by the shore. They've cleared so much of the jungle back that there are no plants for at least half a mile around."

I shook my head. "I've got a lot of work left to do."

I didn't even have to make up the excuse. I really did have a lot of work to do, and my crutch made everything so laboriously slow. Besides, Sirius would be taking Nova, and I didn't know if I could face watching the two of them together.

He reached out, brushing a leaf down my arm. I marveled at how someone so big could be so gentle. "If I help you finish, will you go?"

I touched my arm where the leaf tickled my skin. I did have a lot of work to do, and I didn't want to be alone with that chunk of crystal.

"Deal." I stuck out my hand.

Instead of shaking it, he threaded his large fingers through mine. "What can I do to help?"

"Um…" I glanced down at our intertwined hands. As much as I wanted to hate him, I liked the attention. "The irrigation ditches need to be dug, and all the plants need to be watered."

"That's easy."

I *suppose* digging ditches was easy compared to hauling statue-sized crystals around. Especially if you had superhero muscles. But I didn't appreciate anyone thinking my job was easy. I pulled my hand back and crossed my arms. "Easy when you have both working legs."

"True." He smiled apologetically. "Where do I start?"

I pointed to the corner of the room where Mom stored the gardening tools. Corvus worked quietly, as if it took all of his focus to get the job done. His large hands were steady, leveling the dirt around the base of each plant and threading the hose through the intricate root systems. Mom would be surprised when she checked in the morning.

He walked me back to my family unit on the ship so I could change out of my dirt-stained uniform. As we walked up the ramp above the sloshing water, the need to thank him overcame me.

"You didn't have to help me today. I owe you one."

Corvus shrugged, his broad shoulders moving like a ripple in two mountains. "No problem. I'd finished my work early, so I had the afternoon off."

"Too bad you spent it doing more work." If I'd had the afternoon off, I would have pouted in my room on the *New Dawn* all day.

"I enjoyed spending time with you."

I shot a sideways glance at him. His cheeks reddened and he looked away at the sea, running his hand along the railing. I wondered if he had to try hard to like me or if it came naturally. Before we'd been assigned to one another, I'd hardly spoken a word to him. There was so much I didn't know about him: what he liked and disliked, his goals, and, more important, the shape of his heart.

The question just popped out of my mouth. "Do you think what we're doing here is right?"

He squinted his eyes. "What do you mean?"

"Being here right now, building our lives on Paradise 21?" I kicked a chunk of crystal and it skimmed over the waves before plopping in the water. "It seems unnatural, as if we're taking something that isn't ours to take."

"We have to keep going, Annie." He paused and turned toward me. "If not for the Guide, then for each other."

I wondered if he meant me and him, or our entire ship. Either way, he was right. We owed it to one another to keep life going and build a safe refuge. I thought of Mom and Dad, Grandpapa, Great-grandma Tiff, and all the other Lifers that spent their lives on the ship to get us here. I couldn't let them down.

Corvus had so much strength it radiated out and enveloped me. He'd seemed so simple and dull before, but as I spent more time with him I caught glimpses of an inner resilience and a personality much more profound. If Sirius was mercury, then Corvus was granite, solid and dependable, a person I could latch onto in a time of so much flux. Could I love him?

We entered the ship and he walked me to my family unit.

"Meet you on the dock at sunset?"

I pressed my palm to the panel, and the portal dematerialized. "Sure thing."

He waited, staring at me with an intense, level gaze as the portal re-materialized between us.

"Hanging out with Corvus?" Dad sat at the table, eating leftovers from last night's meal. Now, with the special crystals in the soil, even the leftovers tasted sublime.

"A little." I walked past him to my room.

"He's a great boy. I've heard wonderful things about him from the construction team."

Dad tried to be supportive, but his acceptance of Corvus, when he'd been less than nice to Sirius, irked me. "I've got to go wash up for the festival tonight."

"Sure." Dad pushed a plate over to me. "Make sure you have some dinner first."

I sat down and spooned some rice and steamed peas on my plate. "Where's Mom?"

"She's down in the biodome preparing the remaining seed containers for transfer to the greenhouses."

It hit me again: we really were stuck here, and the ship would soon be left behind, discarded like a shell grown too small. "Shouldn't we keep some here just in case?"

"The engines are failing." Dad suddenly looked years older than middle age. His fork stopped in mid stab, and he placed it down on the plate with a pea the size of a grape impaled on its end. "Once the gears stop spinning, the entire ship will lose power and sink."

Abandoning the ship was the dumbest idea I'd ever heard. What if we needed it for shelter? What if we had to leave Paradise 21? I had to remind myself it wasn't built for another takeoff. "Can't we drag it closer to shore?"

My father shrugged. "What's the point? The ship is beyond repair. Right now we need to focus all our energy on the projects for our future, not the preservation of our past. We've constructed new buildings, established a new home."

A rising feeling of dread squelched my appetite. "What about Grandpapa?"

"We can take out a chunk of the mainframe, enough to keep him alive, and transport him to the shore, but he's growing weaker each day. Even now, he's in the process of appointing a new commander."

I looked down at the peas on my plate. "I want him to live forever. I never want to have to say goodbye like I did to Great-grandma Tiff."

"I know you do." Dad touched my hand gently. "Which is why I'm speaking to you about it now, preparing you for another round of change in our lives. Annie, life *is* change. To deny it is to turn your back on the way of the universe. Grandpapa's bypassed the circle of life for so long. He's grown tired. I know he wants to rest, to put things to an end, as they rightfully should be."

I had no idea how it felt to live through three generations, to cheat death with the help of a machine. It wasn't my place to judge him, yet anger rose inside me and I washed it down with a gulp of water.

"Enough of this sad and dark talk. Go have fun at the festival tonight. Grandpapa still oversees the operations. You still have time to visit him."

"All right." I hadn't spoken with Grandpapa since the argument about Sirius and Corvus. Although I'd forgiven him for not helping me, I'd put off any further visits partly out of embarrassment over my actions and shame for not believing in the system he worked so hard to uphold. I made a mental note to break down those barriers soon, because his days were numbered, just as they were for each one of us.

I managed a few bites before slipping into my favorite long nanofiber dress, and met Corvus on the dock just as the sun set in a lavender blush. I'd let my hair out of its braid and it flowed in crinkly waves down my back. The breeze lifted up stray strands to mingle with the laces of my dress. Despite the doctor's suggestion, I'd left my crutch at home. I flew down the dock, riding on the currents of fate.

Corvus wore a loose-fitting white shirt and civilian microfiber pants. He looked different without his uniform: less of an expectation and more of a person. The wind blew his shirt tight across his back, and I noticed his wide shoulder blades under the thin fabric.

Stop staring before he catches you.

I straightened up, smoothing my hair behind my ear. "Ahem."

Corvus turned from the railing and held out his hand. "Annie, you look gorgeous."

"Thank you." I bowed slightly to acknowledge him. Behind us, colonists tied streamers to the dock posts, the ribbons rustling in the breeze. Tech specialists tested the amps for the music. Hearing the low off-beats made my blood bubble with excitement.

"Come on, they're serving nectar drinks on the beach."

He helped me down the steps of the dock, and my feet sank into the black crystal sand. I followed him to the lapping waves. A swirl of water gushed up to my feet and I hopped backward on my good leg, laughing.

"Close call, huh?" Corvus soaked in the sight of me as if he stared at his dream come alive. The intensity in his eyes made me embarrassed and self-conscious. I turned away, hiding behind the falling veil of my hair.

"I'm not supposed to get the bandages on my ankle wet." I glanced up.

His lips curled in amusement. "A likely excuse."

His teasing made me giggle. "What are they serving at the outpost stand?"

"It's a new juice made from the nectar of the flowers here."

"What does it taste like?"

He raised an eyebrow. "Let's find out." He eyed my bandaged foot. "Why don't you stay here. I'll get us some."

"Okay." I watched him run up the beach and disappear into the crowd. My eyes scanned the congregation. I dreaded the sight of Sirius with Nova, but I couldn't help but wonder if they were happy.

"Where's your crutch?"

I whirled around and there Sirius stood, framed by the setting sun. The breeze tossed his hair around his face. The bridge of his perfect nose was dusted with a bronze glow, as if he'd spent too long outside the ship without his mask.

"I don't need it anymore. My foot feels fine," I lied. My foot ached even as I spoke, but I didn't want to look like a klutz at the festival and remind everyone of my failed attempt to save the colony.

Sirius looked down at the black sand as if I'd told him I didn't need *him* anymore and not the crutch. That would be a lie as well.

"You look beautiful."

"Where's Nova?"

We spoke at the same time, and I didn't have a chance to absorb his compliment or repay it with one of my own.

"She's helping her father finish securing a perimeter fence, just in case."

"In case of what?" My heart sped up. Had someone

else seen the alien?

He gave me a half-smile as if he read my thoughts. "I think it's more to keep us in than it is to keep anything else out."

"What do you mean?"

"Ray's still sick. He's fallen into a deep coma, and the doctors can't bring him out of it."

Guilt seeped in. Here I was enjoying myself while Ray suffered in the emergency bay. How quickly had I forgotten about him? Realization hit me and I cursed Crophaven's subtlety. The festival was a charade, a decoy meant to distract the colonists away from thoughts of danger or death. The last thing we needed was mass hysteria.

"I wish I'd found the answer that day on the mission."

Sirius's face softened into the boy's I once knew so well. "Annie, it's not your fault. You and your mom are doing the best you can to find the source."

"We haven't had much luck doing anything but growing big tomatoes."

"Another important part of our mission here, as dictated by the Guide."

He we were again, talking about the stupid Guide. He sounded like a diplomat and not a friend. I was about to come up with a great, intelligent, witty retort when Sirius's face closed into a stone-hard frown. I turned to see what had upset him so much. Corvus stood behind me, two drinks in hand.

"Sirius."

"Corvus."

The lower workers never got along with the higher command. Corvus was a grunt, and as an aviator Sirius was destined for lieutenant-hood. But I sensed something greater than difference in rank underlying their cold greeting.

"I see you already have your drinks." Although it was mere conversation, Sirius's voice tightened. He held Corvus's stare, as if neither one of them wanted to be the first to look away.

"We have what we need." Corvus glanced down at me and smiled before returning to address Sirius. "You'd best be getting yours."

Behind us, the beat of the music grew louder and the crowd erupted in applause. Sirius bowed and disappeared into the nearest clump of colonists, slithering away in defeat like someone who'd lost a hand at cards.

"You don't get along, do you?" I met his cool blue eyes and refused to look back to where Sirius joined the crowd.

"We have similar interests. Too similar."

I furrowed my eyebrows. I didn't think they had anything in common at all. Before I could respond, the music gained force behind us, and he offered me the drink. "Try it. The juice has tons of vitamin C."

"Great. Just what my ankle needs."

He laughed and took a sip of his drink. I lifted my lips to the cup. The juice flowed down my tongue, reminding me of sweet honey from the beehives in the biodome—a treat only certain colonists got to have on special occasions. I gulped more, wanting the tantalizing sensation to last all night. When I finished, my throat tingled and my belly warmed.

"Wow, you downed the whole thing." Corvus's eyes widened as he looked at me, impressed.

"I guess there's one good thing here on Paradise 21." The bitterness seeped into my voice, surprising me. I couldn't believe how much venom I stored up.

"Come now, I can spot at least one more." Corvus's eyes glittered as he looked into mine. I wondered what else was good on Paradise 21, but he didn't look anywhere special. He just kept staring at me. He took my hand.

"Let's go dance."

"My foot—"

"I'll make sure you don't put pressure on it."

And he did. Putting a strong arm around my waist, he hoisted me into the air and back down again in a pirouette. We spun together and I laughed, my hair catching in my mouth. He brushed it back and smoothed his thumb over my lips. My heart thudded against my chest, and I wondered if it was because of the exertion or something more.

A scream pierced through the techno beat and the music stopped abruptly. I turned around as the crowd grew silent. Nova broke through the jungle, holding a young girl in her arms.

"Who is it?" I whispered, standing on tiptoe to get a closer look.

Colonists surrounded her and took the girl from her arms. Lieutenant Crophaven pushed his way through the crowd. "Take the girl to the emergency bay." He turned to Nova. "What happened?"

"I found her lying face-down in the jungle. She was unresponsive, so I picked her up and brought her here."

Crophaven had that official annoyed look he did so well. "Come with me. You need to be examined as well for any contagion."

He turned to address the crowd and his eyes skimmed over mine with recognition. "For the rest of the colony, don't panic. We'll postpone the celebration until further notice. Return to your family units. If anyone here has any strange symptoms, report to sick bay immediately."

A line formed to the ship with people whispering in scared tones. I followed Corvus and joined in behind a bunch of younger teens. "Do you think she has what Ray has?"

He shrugged. "I don't know. I hope Nova's all right

and didn't catch anything from the girl."

Why would he be so worried about Nova?

I blocked my brain from going further down that path. I wouldn't allow myself to think about what would happen to Sirius if his assigned lifemate grew sick and died.

CHAPTER TWELVE

VISITOR

My locator beeped with an incoming message. I checked the sender and slumped down, pressing the receive button with resignation.

When can I see you again?

Corvus. Would he ever give up? Probably not. He'd persisted all morning, and I needed more time to sort out my feelings.

The crystal flickered in the back of the greenhouse. My other problem. Why couldn't everyone, including the aliens, just leave me alone?

I ignored both distractions, pruning the tomato vines, hoping the play of light was a hovercraft in the sky. My imagination ran on overdrive due to a night of fitful sleep. Anxiety crept up my spine like a ventilator spider, prickling the hair on my back with spindly legs. I was thankful Corvus had finished the brunt of my work the previous day. All I had to do was check that the new irrigation tubes spouted enough water and grind more crystals for the soil.

Too much had happened the night before, and my mind wrestled with the thought of Ray lying in the emergency bay with the little girl, the thought of Nova falling ill as well, and the thought of Corvus as more than a friend. These unresolved feelings churned in my stomach in a foul brew, and I could hardly keep down the few slices of pear I'd stuffed into my mouth before leaving for my work.

The light reflecting off the crystal gained intensity, casting rainbows across the ceiling. I couldn't ignore it any longer. Holding my breath, I crept down the row of tomato plants. The stems towered over me, reminding me of the jungle.

The crystal's light throbbed as I approached. I smoothed my fingers over the sleek surface, wondering why the hell I didn't run away screaming. Guess my curiosity won over fear.

The locator beeped on my arm. I'd fallen into the habit of turning the life-form scan on every day when I worked alone, hoping it would alert me if any strange aliens decided to show up and take their crystal back.

A figure approached the greenhouse, skinnier and taller than Mom. Because of the mask she wore, I couldn't recognize her, and I rose to open the portal with shaky fingers. I pulled back the glass separating us and she rounded the bend, staring at me with blazing emerald eyes framed in hair so lustrous it burned like fire in the purple sun.

"Nova, are you all right?"

She pulled down the mask and said the first words she'd ever said to my face. "I'm perfectly fine."

"The girl wasn't contagious?"

A flicker of irritation crossed her eyes. "No, Amber Woods didn't infect me."

We stood at the threshold like two statues. I blocked the entrance, and she stood too far away to step in. The moment couldn't have been more awkward had we been naked.

I swallowed hard and scrounged up some kind words. "Come in. Make yourself comfortable."

"Thank you." She didn't sound thankful at all.

I gestured for her to sit on a metal chair by the lab table, but she waved me away. "I won't be long. No one knows I'm here."

"Oh." I couldn't imagine why she'd come, besides to taunt me. I wanted to scream *You have Sirius. What else could you possibly want?* I held my tongue against the side of my mouth and gritted my teeth. There must be a reason why she finally decided to talk to little old me after all these years.

"I found something with Amber in the jungle." Her eyes darted around the greenhouse as if spies lurked in every corner.

I followed her gaze but only saw the large hulk of purple crystal casting a shadow on the far back wall. "No one's here. Go on."

Nova pulled a cloth out of her pocket and unfolded it. "When I found her, she was holding this."

I peered down into the fabric, my heart racing. A flower, bright as crimson, red as newly shed blood lay against the white micro-fabric. Its star-shaped petals curved inward, and a small pod lay at its center.

"What is it?" Because I was supposed to be an authority on plants, embarrassment flushed in my cheeks.

"I thought you could find out." Nova refolded the fabric and placed it on the lab table. "Sirius told me you and your mom are working on finding out what made Ray sick. He said if anyone would know what to do with it, it would be you." Nova shook her head. "I didn't want the other scientists getting their hands on it. They've been keeping too much from us, and I need to know the truth."

I stepped back in awe, looking at Nova, who'd changed from a haughty princess to a renegade. She trusted me with her specimen. She actually thought I could help more than anyone else on Paradise 21?

"Did Sirius put you up to this?"

She blinked and looked away momentarily, biting her lower lip. A hint of jealousy passed through her eyes. Why was she jealous of me? She was the one who had him.

"Yes, Sirius recommended bringing this sample to you. I respect his faith in you, so I agreed." She squirmed a little, as if she wasn't comfortable saying so much.

I opened my mouth and gawked, speechless. Maybe I didn't know her as well as I thought. Besides that, Nova handed me an enormous responsibility. The scared part of me wanted to turn it in to Lieutenant Crophaven, but an even greater part wanted to dissect it with tweezers and battle this damn planet with my own two hands. I met her gaze. "Thank you for bringing this to me."

"Don't thank me." Nova cast a glance over her shoulder just as another figure walked by the smoky glass. She jogged to the portal. "Just find a cure."

After she left, I strapped on my bio mask and pulled a chair over to the table to study the petals under the microscope. Despite their striking color, nothing separated them from anything else on Paradise 21. I turned my examination over to the pod at the center. Using a scalpel, I cut a small incision in the outer membrane. White fluid bled out like pus from a sore. I scraped a sample onto a plastic microscope tray and slipped it under the lens.

Tiny crawling microbes writhed. I clicked a higher resolution for more magnification, and gasped. The little buggers looked more like parasites than any pollen I'd ever seen. With squirming, spidery legs and pincher jaws, they barreled down into the plastic, trying to gnarl their way through.

Were they infecting the plant? Or did they coexist in a symbiotic relationship? More important, were they the cause of the infection?

I used my locator to send a message to Mom. Her

locator buzzed back as temporarily unreachable, so I typed *top priority, come ASAP* and returned my attention to the slide under the lens. The microorganisms' movements slowed until they stopped and died. They couldn't exist outside the plant host. So how could they travel through the air and infect us?

Had Amber eaten the pod? I shook my head. She'd have to be pretty stupid to put anything from Paradise 21 in her mouth, and Ray wouldn't ever ingest something he found on a scouting mission. No. There was a missing link.

I looked down at the dead microbes and felt as though I stared at one of those puzzle pictures, barely making out the shape but not knowing what it was. Maybe it wasn't the source of the infection at all. Maybe she just found a pretty flower in the jungle, one with nasty little bug things squirming in its belly.

I stood to test the petals in chemical samples when the crystal at the far end of the greenhouse cast a strange glow, emanating pulses of light between the tomato leaves.

"Oh, jeez." I slapped my hand over the mask covering my mouth. This time I wasn't staying around. I backed toward the exit of the greenhouse and my foot caught the leg of the stool. I toppled over, and the stool clanged against the table legs, making the most racket I ever heard in my life. The glow sparkled as it moved through the rows of tomato plants, illuminating the far reaches of the domed ceiling with flickering light.

This was it for me. The aliens had come to catch the person who'd stolen their crystal, and they'd find me red-handed, scurrying backward on my butt. How could I tell them it wasn't my fault, that I didn't even want Mom to grind the crystal into powder, that I lamented the death of the jungle as the Landrovers tore it down?

The silhouette of the head and bumpy wings came into focus as the alien rounded the corner, and my stomach clutched into a tight ball. *How did it get into the greenhouse?*

It lifted its bony hand, fingers longer than my arms. I cringed back, hiding behind my elbow. "Take it. Take the crystal. I don't care."

The alien didn't point to the crystal. His fingers waved over the lab table and his palm hovered over the red flower. As the brittle fingers came to rest, its other hand spread out before me in three branch-like appendages. The alien held the position in the air, and then the fingers closed in like a curled-up spider.

I lowered my arm and squinted against the bright light. "I don't understand."

The life-form locator beeped, making me jump. The alien backed away and I reached out. "Wait." There were so many questions I had to ask.

The portal to the greenhouse slid open and I faced a waft of jungle air. Mom panted in the threshold, tearing off her mask. "What is it, Andromeda? Are you okay?"

"Mom, look!" I pointed in the direction of the alien, but when I turned my head around, the row between the tomato plants lay empty. The crystal didn't even flicker anymore.

Mom's concern for me morphed into annoyance. "Look at what? I left a very important meeting to answer your distress call."

Where could it have gone so quickly? I could chase after it, but I didn't want to be taken back to the emergency bay. I decided not to mention the alien. "Nova brought in a sample from the jungle, a flower Amber Woods carried when she fell ill."

Mom's eyes widened. "Have you taken a look at it?"

I nodded, sniffing back tears. The alien sighting made me want to crawl into my sleep pod and curl up forever.

"What did you find?"

My legs wobbled so much I couldn't bring myself up

from the floor, so I pointed to the microscope. "Take a look for yourself."

As Mom rushed to the lab table, I scanned the room for any trace of the alien. There were no tracks in the soil where it had approached me, and the crystal lay silent, reflecting the purplish rays of morning sun like an innocent bystander.

"Turn off that damn life-form scan." Mom brought up a stool and positioned the microscope in both hands. I hadn't noticed it was still beeping. I pressed the button on my arm and the screen went blank.

"Wow, I've never seen this before." Mom glued her eye to the lens. "Do you have any live samples?"

"Scrape the inside of the flower pod."

As I picked up the small device in my hands, I turned off the insistent beep and checked the history. I realized only two beings besides me had registered on the scanner that morning: Nova and Mom.

Mom's hand jutted out and she wiggled her fingers. "Annie, get me the scalpel."

I could only stand, numb and confused.

No one else could find the aliens because they didn't register on the life-form locator. That meant they had no heat signature, no mass, and cast no seismic vibrations. Was it a hologram? A projection cast by the crystal glow? If so, where was their homeland? Why were they contacting me?

"Annie?"

I shook my head and reached over for the scalpel, handing the slim metal instrument to Mom with shaky fingers. "What if another race colonized Paradise 21?"

"That's improbable, almost impossible." Mom took the scalpel and grazed the inside of the pod. "None of Old Earth's thousands of scout ships ever found another intelligent species. The odds of another race able to navigate space like us are slim, and the odds of them finding the exact same planet we found are even less. What we have to worry about is these little creatures squirming under the microscope. If one of them gets into our system, it may create havoc. It may be the culprit we're looking for."

Her voice held so much hope I couldn't undermine the discovery with crazy stories of alien holograms. Instead, I righted the metal stool and sank onto it, deep in thought. If no one would help me find the aliens, I'd have to go looking for them by myself.

CHAPTER THIRTEEN

FORGOTTEN CITY

"Goodnight, Mom. I'm going back to the ship." I stood up and rubbed my bleary eyes.

Mom didn't even look up from the microscope. "Tell your dad I'm staying here for the night. There's still too much we don't know."

"I will." Although I doubted he'd still be awake. Every night he collapsed in his sleep pod seconds after wolfing down dinner. Paradise 21 plagued all of us in its own way, making us eager fools, lifeless zombies, and paranoid delusionalists. The planet tore my family apart, and I resented it.

I pressed the button with an agitated sigh and the greenhouse portal closed behind me. As I took my first step out into the night, something reached out from the darkness and grabbed my arm. I struggled, my voice catching. I always thought I'd be able to scream in an emergency, yet fear stuffed its way down my throat, making me mute. A large hand closed on my arm. I realized it was no alien or plant tentacle. I yanked backward until the shadow stepped into the diaphanous light of Paradise 21's twin moons.

"Corvus! What are you doing?"

He put a finger to his lips and shushed me. His voice was barely a whisper. "Come on. I have something you have to see."

Before I could reply, he gestured behind him to the back of the greenhouse where neither moon's rays could reach. My feet stuck to the ground in a moment of indecision. Adventures always got me in trouble.

He hissed into the night. "We have to go before someone sees us."

My heart thumped against my bio-suit. Could I trust him? How well did I know him, really? Everything about the jungle night screamed danger: the glare of two alien moons, the thick, murky darkness, and the putrid stink of the turf in the twilight's leftover dew. Corvus was a beacon of solidarity, a symbol of everything wholesome in my world. Sometimes I hated him for it, but other times his strength drew me in like a planet to the sun.

"Okay." I followed him behind the greenhouse, ducking underneath the rain gutters to avoid being seen in the moonlight.

Corvus spoke over his shoulder as he led me forward. "I've been waiting for hours. I thought you'd never come out."

"You could have buzzed me with your locator."

He stopped and turned around to meet my eyes. "Yours must be broken. You don't answer my messages."

I looked away guiltily. "I haven't had time. We're working overtime on finding a cure for Ray and Amber."

"Oh." Corvus nodded and continued on, rounding a bend. He slipped down an incline to the most recent construction site. The equipment poked up through the hole in the turf like the discarded toys of a giant toddler. In the dark, the area seemed abandoned and forbidden.

Corvus jumped down the ledge, but I couldn't follow.

"Wait." The toes of my boots teetered on the edge. "If I'm going to follow you down that hole and risk being caught, then I should know where you're taking me." I never had the guts to demand it of Sirius, but with Corvus I wasn't afraid of being myself. So what if he didn't like the real me?

Corvus turned around with an eager look in his eyes, as though he couldn't wait another minute. He nodded, agreeing that what I'd said was fair, and walked back toward me. His eyes shone wide in the moonlight.

"They found something."

I leaned over the ledge to get a better look at his features in the finicky light. "What do you mean?"

Corvus sighed. "I'm not supposed to tell anyone outside the construction team, but I wanted to show you because you saw something in the jungle that very first day, and it might be connected."

Now he had my full attention. I plunged down the ledge. "What did they find?"

Corvus caught me as I slid down. "Ruins."

My mind whirled. "Like the pyramids on Old Earth? Or the Coliseum of Ancient Rome before terrorists blew it up?"

"Not quite. These buildings are...stranger." Corvus grabbed my hand and I squeezed back, borrowing his strength as he pulled me deeper into the excavation site.

Beyond the cranes and piles of rotting turf, turret-shaped shadows jutted up from the black crystal sand. Corvus reached into the front seat of a Landrover and pulled out a light. "I think we're far enough in. No one should see the beacon."

After smacking it against his hand a few times, the light flickered on, illuminating a field of spiraling ivory-white turret tops. The carrot-shaped structures were too impossibly slender for human buildings, with pinprick tops reaching toward the sky.

"Wow." Words failed me. There must have been twenty of them, spread out in a cylindrical shape. Only the crowns were visible above the black crystal, and I wanted to run to the base of the first one and dig with my bare hands to see what lay beneath the sand.

I jogged over and smoothed my hands over the ivory, exploring the perfectly shaped curves. The surface felt cold and slick to my touch, like the metal walls in the *New Dawn*, but it gleamed shiny as polished opal in the moonlight, much prettier than chrome.

Corvus pulled me ahead. "There's more."

Dumpsters filled with black crystal littered the dig site. We walked through them to the last tower in the back. The crystals had been removed around its base, and we slid down the incline to an arched window. Corvus shined his light inside the building. Hulky shapes cast ominous shadows.

"I should go first." Corvus suddenly looked at me as if I'd snap my ankle again. "Just in case."

The thought should have annoyed me, but I was too scared to go in by myself. "I'm right behind you."

We stepped around chunks of crystal bigger than my head. I imagined Mom rubbing her hands together in glee. Oh, how the tomatoes would grow!

The archway was still halfway buried, so we had to duck and crawl underneath the threshold. Once my head cleared the entrance, I stood up and brushed my bio-suit off. Corvus's light flickered over high tables melting up from the floor like skinny mushrooms above our heads. I followed him deeper into the structure until he stopped abruptly. I fell against him, my hands clutching his muscled shoulder blades.

"What's wrong?" I pulled away, embarrassed to be touching him in the dark.

"I'm not sure you should see this anymore." Guilt

tinged his voice. His shoulders sagged.

Anger rumbled up inside me. "What? You drag me all the way down here into these alien ruins and then decide I can't see what comes next?"

He turned around. "I don't want to scare you."

"I'm fine. I can handle it." I tried to speak with an even voice, but his hesitation frightened me more than I wanted to admit.

He pulled his bio mask off his face and ran a hand over his short blond hair. "When I heard about this, you were the first person that came to mind, and I counted the hours until my shift ended and I could sneak by the greenhouses. Now I wonder if this was more what I wanted for myself." His eyes sparkled like two blue sapphires. "For us to be down here together, alone, on an adventure. I didn't think about if it would make you happy."

"Nonsense, Corvus." I tried to comfort him and touched his arm, wrapping my fingers around his bicep and giving it a squeeze. Sirius used to drag me all over the place with him, but he never gave a thought about if I wanted to go. Here was "the oaf", as I used to call him, thinking about my feelings. It almost melted my heart. "This is exactly where I want to be right now."

His eyes flashed back at me, making me blush. Feeling as though I misled him, I cleared my throat. "I need answers, and this place may have what I'm looking for."

Corvus frowned but quickly covered it up. "All right. I sure hope it has what you need."

I wanted to say something more reassuring, but he'd already turned around. He hoisted the beacon light and shone it down on the floor in front of him. Lumps cluttered the smooth surface, as if the ivory had crusted over with fallen debris.

Disappointment crashed through me. I thought I'd

get some answers. "I don't see anything."

Corvus stepped beside me, our shoulders touching. "Look closer."

I leaned down. Three long fingers stretched out toward my foot: a hand.

"Fossils," I whispered, crouching over the remains.

The hand extended back to a long skinny arm, the bones slim as a bird's legs, in the shape of a fallen angel with broken wings. I reached down to touch the crusty skeleton, and shivers scurried down my spine.

"Is this what you saw in the jungle that day?"

I put my five fingers over the three-fingered hand and traced up along the arm bone to the wings. Large eye sockets filled with crystal dust stared back at me with the same expression I saw in the jungle. "Yes, I'm sure of it."

"Annie, you're not crazy at all, and this proves it."

My head swam in deep waters, questions surfacing like ugly sea creatures with spiky teeth. "But this civilization must have died centuries ago. The alien in the jungle was alive."

"Maybe they have another base somewhere else on this planet?" Corvus shone the light around the room but we didn't see any signs of recent life.

"Don't you think the ship's scavenge droids would have found it? They scoured every inch of the planet before we landed."

"They also didn't find anything that would make us sick, and now look at poor Ray."

I shook my head. Something about this puzzle didn't add up. "A microbe can be easily overlooked, but an entire civilization?"

Corvus shrugged. "Maybe they left, and now they're back."

CHAPTER FOURTEEN

ANSWERS

When I woke the next morning I buzzed Mom with my locator. *Don't feel well. Taking the day off.*

She'd be frustrated at the timing of it, with the microbe samples dangling right before her eyes and no assistant to jot down the readings, but I had to alert someone of our findings and it had to be a person I could trust, someone who wouldn't get Corvus and me in deeper trouble.

I buzzed my grandpapa on the intercom, but he didn't answer. Making sure Dad had already gone to work, I snuck out of our family unit and took the elevator to the main control deck. I hadn't heard from my grandpapa in a long time.

Was he still alive?

I reminded myself if the *New Dawn* still ran, then he was up there somewhere, watching over us, keeping us safe. When I closed my eyes, he surrounded me in a guiding force through the buzzing hum of the lights and the smooth lift of the platform below my feet. I hadn't seen him since our last argument about my lifemate, and I was ready to tell him I was sorry.

The portal dematerialized and I stepped into the corridor, smoothing out my uniform to look presentable. If anyone would believe me, my grandpapa would. He wouldn't report Corvus for taking me to the dig site. I had to tell him the aliens matched the bones in the excavation. The upper command needed to know the strange winged beings were still out there, still alive, spying on our colonization attempts.

The guards stood in my way like pieces lined up on a chess board. Usually they recognized me and parted as I walked toward them. Today they stared over me as if I were invisible.

"It's Andromeda Barliss." I emphasized my last name. "I'm here to see my grandpapa."

"Sorry, kid." A man in his early forties, the same age as my dad, spoke up. "He's not taking visitors."

"Not even from his own great-granddaughter?"

The man shook his head. "Nope. He's preparing the ship for evacuation."

I tried to keep my voice steady, but it rose to almost a shriek in my throat. "Already? We're not scheduled to leave the ship until the housing modules are assembled."

The man's eyes looked kind, but his compassion did nothing to appease me. "It's a long process, disconnecting all the systems, transferring the data to computers on the colony site."

I peered over his shoulder at the chrome portal, imaging my grandpapa in his control chair, just a mere few feet away. "You have to let me through. I have findings to report."

"Take your findings to Lieutenant Crophaven. Commander Barliss has appointed him as the new leader in charge of colonization." The man gripped his laser across his chest and resumed his stance, as if to say our conversation had ended. I stood there like a dumb desert cow from Sahara 354, staring off into space. Or I guess it wasn't space anymore, but Paradise 21 beyond the sight panels.

Lieutenant Crophaven wouldn't listen to me any more

than he'd listened to Mom that day in the emergency room. He'd have me and Corvus taken in for seclusion before we spread the word and panic ensued. What was I going to do? Without my grandpapa in charge I was a nobody. Turning away from the guards, I dragged my feet down the corridor in defeat.

When I returned to my family unit, a message beeped on the main wallscreen. My pulse accelerated as I thought of Mom's angry face, or Lieutenant Crophaven's stern grimace. Did they discover our footprints at the dig site?

I walked over with my backpack still on and pressed the button with quivery fingers.

Sirius's handsome features graced my wallscreen like a teen idol. I smoothed back my hair, suddenly aware of my lack of a shower, but I realized it was a prerecorded message.

"Annie, I'm going on my first flight mission tomorrow at dawn. I'm not sure how long I'll be away. I wanted to tell you because I didn't want to leave without saying goodbye. I'll be at the airstrip all day practicing routine landings and tactical maneuvers if you want to stop by."

I stared at the wallscreen for several minutes after the message ended and the pixels went black. Did I want to say goodbye? Should I?

I searched my feelings and came up with a mixture of anger, lust, and regret. What if he died on this mission and I never got a chance to see him again?

Corvus's cool blue eyes and easy smile intruded my thoughts, questioning the yearning cravings of my wanton heart. He'd done so much for me. Would he mind if I visited Sirius? I'd only meet him to say goodbye, and I had the day off anyway because I'd called in sick.

After a quick shower, I strapped on my bio mask, grabbed my backpack, and exited the *New Dawn*, heading toward the newly paved airstrip at the far end of the colony. Corsairs whizzed in the sky above my head, silver birds against a violet canvas of filtered sunlight.

I walked through the stationary transport ships to the faster, lighter air gliders perched on the edge of the jungle turf. Lieutenant Crophaven stared at me with a shifty eye as I approached. I wondered if he could see into my mind and pick apart my innermost secrets.

"Where are you going, young lady?"

Here was my chance to come clean. I could spew up every truth into his hard-edged face: hoarding the flower specimen, sneaking into the excavation site, seeing aliens. I straightened as tall as I could, but the top of my head only reached the broad curve of his chest. "I'm here to say goodbye to my friend, Sirius Smith. He's going on a mission tomorrow at dawn."

"Ah, yes. Andromeda, Delta Barliss's daughter? Is that right? How's the ankle?"

Why did he have to remind me of my failure? Did he only see me as a troublemaker?

"It's fine. Thank you." Silently, I told the pain to stop, but it burned all the way up my leg.

He read his locator. "I'm afraid he's up in the air right now, but he'll be down shortly. You're more than welcome to wait on the perimeter, where it's safer for civilians."

"Okay." I wanted to flee the lieutenant's penetrating gaze before something slipped out, so I ducked my head in salute and ran to the edge of the airstrip, where the pavement ended in jungle vines. Discarded cartons of supplies lay in a heap on the edge of the turf. I upended one and sat on top of it, kicking my legs back and forth against the plastic container.

Thump-thump. Thump-thump.

I wondered what to say to Sirius. What would he say back? A small voice inside me dreaded the conversation, but a much louder urge commanded me to see him.

A Corsair glided down effortlessly, hovered above my head, and landed on the airstrip. The hatch opened and the aviator jumped out, light as an acrobat. My heart sped. He shook off his helmet and exposed a head of curly blond hair. Nope. Not Sirius. I settled back down, biting my fingernails. Waiting was the hardest part of life. The entire population of the *New Dawn*, except for me, waited for Paradise 21. Now here I was waiting for a future that could never be.

A strange blur of light distracted me from my melancholy thoughts. I turned my head, shielding my eyes against the glare of the dark plum rays of the noonday sun. A figure stood on the edge of the turf, apart from the aviators congregating around a large transport ship. His hand rose and he waved in my direction. I looked behind me, but no one was there. He must be trying to get my attention. Was it Sirius? Had I missed his landing? I squinted against the light, looking for that familiar dark swash of hair.

This man's hair was light brown and thin. Ray? No, it couldn't be. What was he doing outside the ship? With his mask off as well. You'd think that boy had learned his lesson the first time he wandered in the jungle. Not only that, but it looked as though a transport ship prepared for takeoff just a few feet away, and he stood too close.

I called his name out at the top of my lungs. He gestured over his shoulder and disappeared into the jungle.

"Wait!"

I jumped off the supply container. A hundred questions bombarded my mind. I ran by a transport ship just as the engines roared, and crystal dust surrounded me in a plume. I pushed through the haze, batting my arms at the cloudy air until my feet fell on the turf. I entered the jungle where Ray disappeared, pushing the vines out of my way.

Large crystals jutted up from the turf like weeds in a garden. I weaved my way around them and called out Ray's name over the din of the transport's engines.

"I'm sorry. I had to get you closer to the crystals so we could talk."

I whirled around, startled. Ray leaned on one of the larger quartz formations. The purple sun filtered down through the vines and cast him in a violet, otherworldly light.

"What are you doing out here?"

"Trying to get your attention."

"Shouldn't you be on the ship?"

He shook his head. "Not anymore."

All the questions in my mind froze and I stood there not knowing what to make of it. Although I didn't know him very well, Ray seemed quieter, more at peace. Maybe it was just the way the sun's light hit him, but his uniform looked brighter and hazy, like my eyes had glazed over. Maybe they had.

"Listen carefully, Annie. They tried to warn me, and now I'm trying to warn you."

I nodded and focused my concentration away from the roar of the transport ships taking off behind us.

"Something big is going to happen beyond that ridge. I'm not sure what it is exactly, but it has to do with what made me sick. You have to send a team to investigate, or the entire colony may be at risk."

"What do you mean? Why are you telling me?" I jabbed my finger over my shoulder. "Lieutenant Crophaven is right over there. He's the one in charge of operations now."

Ray blinked, and his body swayed before he caught himself, clinging to the crystal as if it gave him strength. "I've tried but he won't listen. You're the only one sensitive to the crystal vibrations, Annie." He leaned forward and his eyes glistened. "You can see."

"See what?"

Engines roared behind us as a transport ship rose from the ground. The wind ripped through the jungle like a hurricane and debris whipped through the air. A vine the size of Lieutenant Crophaven's thigh came at me, smacking me in the face.

I fell with a crunch to the turf. The clangor of the engines muted and the purple light of the jungle went black..

AUBRIE DIONNE

CHAPTER FIFTEEN

WARNING

Billions of stars surrounded me, winking and blinking in foreign constellations. I soared in space like an eagle from Old Earth, with my arms spread out like wings. It wasn't cold, like the astrophysicists said it would be, and I could breathe wondrous clean air, not the stink of Paradise 21.

Worlds passed below me, barren desert planets, icy chunks of tundra and hard crusted rock. Only one planet glowed green and blue. I accelerated to it, reaching out with open arms. As the orb grew bigger, the blue and green blossomed into gray plumes of soot and ash. I was too late. Several generations too late. All I had left was my purple planet where I started, the strange and dangerous world of aliens and vines.

As I turned to go back, a splinter of white vaulted through space in a cylindrical comet with a single trajectory. I pushed toward it, hoping and dreading what it was.

A coffin. Not any coffin, but one from the New Dawn. *As I met its speed with my own, I recognized the smooth microfiber and the emblem of a ship cutting through high seas. It could be any of a number of colonists discarded for six generations as the ships coursed to their paradise destinations. Somehow, I knew this coffin was unlike all the others. This one held Great-grandma Tiff.*

119

I reached down and scraped away the crystal formations on the sight panel, expecting a withered corpse inside. My great-grandma lay as though she slept and dreamed, with rosy cheeks and soft, wrinkled skin. Her white hair crowned her head in light wisps, and her tiny mouth pouted in a thoughtful frown.

I grabbed the casket and held onto it, hugging it with my arms and slowing down both our speeds to a standstill. We floated together in the deep backdrop of space. Without a second thought, I snapped open the sight panel with my bare hands and a whoosh of stale air came out.

"Why couldn't you live long enough to see Paradise 21?" I asked as if she could answer me through the dark embrace of death. Great-grandma Tiff's eyelids fluttered, and I wondered if deep space breathed. Her eyes opened and a smile broke upon her face. "I didn't want to, my dear Annie. I had a complete life and then some. I was relieved to see it end."

"I need you now more than ever. Paradise 21 is so confusing. My life is changing fast, and I have so many decisions to make."

She nodded, as if the troubles in life were inevitable. "Be true to yourself. Search your feelings to find out who you really are. Many years I lived as a tough spitfire with ruthless renegades in Pirate Central, and that wasn't truly who I was. I longed for a stable life, a loving husband. Only when I realized it did I find my place in the universe, my seat on the New Dawn.*"*

Buzzing filled my ears, and I shook my head to ward it out. "The New Dawn *isn't flying anymore. Soon we'll have to abandon it."*

"You must learn to let go." I could barely hear her through the insistent humming. I squeezed my eyes shut, and the blackness of space seeped in.

***

I awoke groggy and with my head pounding. Another whoosh of wind as a transport ship left the airstrip beyond the jungle perimeter. The vine that smacked me in the face dangled inches from my nose, tickling my cheek with its curly end. How long had I been out?

120

The sunlight filtered through the canopy of vines in a ruddy violet blue, which meant early evening. Had I slept here all day? Why hadn't Ray called for help? Maybe he was hurt as well.

I hoisted myself up and searched the turf for Ray. Vines, vines, and more vines twisted up against the crystal outcroppings, but no sign of Ray. I hoped he was all right. Only a real jerk would leave a girl unconscious in the jungle, and that wasn't Ray's style. I'd have to check on him once I got back to the *New Dawn*.

Brushing my knees off, I made my way back to the airstrip. The Corsairs were parked for the night in a fleet of rows as if they guarded the edge of the jungle. I pulled on the shoulder of the first man I found and asked about Sirius.

"The aviators have all gone back to the *New Dawn*." He rubbed a metal cylinder with a cloth. Oil stained his shirt. "They have a long day ahead of them tomorrow. Have to be up well before dawn."

I knew that much, but I thanked the man and jogged back toward the ship, thoughts rolling around in my head much resembling the thunder clouds closing in above me for a nightly rainstorm. The air fizzled with static electricity, and I wondered if it had anything to do with what was to come.

The corridors of the *New Dawn* bustled with activity. Everyone rushed home early to avoid the rainstorm. I pushed my way through to my family unit, flashed my wrist locator, and waited for the portal to dissolve.

"Andromeda, you're late. Are you okay?" Mom chopped enormous vegetables on the kitchen counter with the same laser knife she took out scouting with her that very first day. Her voice and squinty eyes had more than a hint of suspicion in them. I'd hoped she'd still be in the greenhouses, but unfortunately for me this was one of the rare evenings she came home early to make dinner.

"I'm fine. I went for a walk to clear my head." A simmer of annoyance sped through me. Here I was trying to save the colony, and everything I did looked irresponsible.

"You don't look well. What's that red bump on your cheek?" Mom walked over and put her hand on my forehead.

Telling her I went to see Sirius and stumbled into the path of a transport ship didn't seem like a great idea. "Um…I fell on the way."

"You shouldn't be out and about if you're not feeling well. I see you didn't take your crutch." She gave me a stern glance.

I scrunched up my face. "I'm fine, really, and my ankle's much better."

"Okay then." She sighed like I plagued her with a thousand woes and handed me silverware. "Here, help me set the table."

"For three?" My voice rose in hope.

"For two. Your dad's working late."

"When can we all sit together at the table again as a family?" My voice came out whinier than I would've liked. "Andromeda, you know how important these first months are on Paradise 21. We must establish ourselves if we're going to succeed as a colony. A lot of work has to be done, and your dad is an important part of the power systems team."

All I wanted was for her to say she missed our previous life, too. But she'd never utter a word of that. Not my mom. Besides, she was probably happier now than ever.

"I learned more about the microbes today," Mom offered, probably trying to change the subject.

"Oh, really?"

"Although they're antibiotic-resistant, I'm developing a strain that may weaken their defenses."

"That's great, Mom." I had a sudden pang of guilt for calling in sick. As important as it was to find out more about the microbes, I had to find those aliens. Then I thought of my conversation with Ray. He'd said "they." Did he mean the aliens as well? I still needed to find out what happened to him.

"Hey, Mom, have you seen Ray?"

Mom dropped the napkin holder on the table and stared at me as if I'd grown another head. "That's a cruel joke. Honestly, I don't know what's gotten into you lately." Her voice stung, and I shook my head. "What?"

"Didn't you hear?" Mom's brow creased.

"No, I didn't hear anything. Why?"

"Ray died early this morning. He fell deeper into the coma and they couldn't keep his heart rate steady."

It was impossible: I saw him alive and well in the jungle. He talked to me.

"Andromeda, are you okay?"

"No." The silverware slipped from my fingers and clanged on the table. Mom moved to comfort me, but I tore myself from her grasp and flew into my room. I banged my fist against the wall panel and the portal materialized in between us.

I was afraid Mom would override the portal lock and barge in, but I heard no sounds from the kitchen. She probably left to get Dad.

Tears ran down my face as I tried to put my world back together and still have it make sense. If Ray was dead, what had I seen in the jungle? His ghost?

That was such a ridiculous thought, it almost made me laugh. Maybe he escaped and they were trying to cover it up. Maybe I was out for longer than I thought and I talked to him before he died. Then I remembered he was in a coma, so that wouldn't make sense. Nothing made sense.

I thought about the aliens. Our scanners couldn't

detect them. They were transparent. I always saw them around crystals. Maybe they did something to Ray to make his body transparent. How? If he'd died, how would they have his body? That made me think about ghosts again, but this time it didn't seem as ridiculous.

Ray said we needed to talk next to the crystals, so maybe they gave off some sort of psionic pulse, allowing the spirit realm to come through. I wished more than ever Great-grandma Tiff was still alive. Everyone onboard the ship thought paranormal stuff was nonsense, but Great-grandma Tiff used to tell me psychic ability ran in our family. She hinted at her own inklings from time to time. In fact, wasn't she talking about that the evening before she died?

Thinking about Great-grandma Tiff's death complicated everything, so I pushed that thought aside. I needed to focus on what happened to Ray. If he really was a ghost, then were the aliens all dead? Did I see the ghosts of their failed civilization? Were they trying to warn me, like Ray said?

All this time I thought they were the enemy, and here they were trying to help me, to get me to see before the same thing happened to all of us. How could I be so prejudiced?

The puzzle came together before my eyes: the aliens, Ray's ghost, the warnings. If what Ray said was true, something endangered our colony beyond that ridge, and I was the only one who knew about it, the only one who could stop it.

I threw my arms up and paced my room. What could a lowly species integration assistant do? No one would listen to my story without throwing me in the emergency sick bay. I had no way of getting beyond that ridge.

I stopped in mid-step and froze.

I knew someone who could.

CHAPTER SIXTEEN

MISSION FAREWELL

Dawn broke the horizon in a soft display of pale orchid light. I ran from the ship's loading dock to the airstrip, hoping with a bursting heart I wasn't too late. Every ship in the air might be Sirius's and their roaring engines mocked my feeble plight. I had to wait until both my parents left our family unit or risk being bombarded by a slew of questions. I wasn't ready to tell anyone where I was headed, or why.

A laser of pain shot through my ankle every time I stomped on it, but I clenched my teeth and closed the distance, putting myself once again under the stern gaze of Lieutenant Crophaven.

"Here to see Sirius Smith again?"

Panting, I struggled to answer him. "Yes. I couldn't find him yesterday."

"Well, you're in luck. The mission was delayed due to a faulty engine capacitor. They won't be leaving for another few hours."

Relief flooded my body, and I felt like I'd liquefy right on the spot. "Where is he?"

"Over there by his Corsair. Keep your conversation short and don't distract him. He's got a tough scouting mission on his hands."

"Yes, sir." As if anything I had to say would calm him down?

I jogged over to the row of ships, looking for his familiar head of space-black hair. The ships all looked the same to me and I didn't know his unit number, so I wandered around.

The paint was so new, each Corsair looked like a child's toy, polished up for pretend missions. I touched the airbrushed symbol of the *New Dawn*, tracing the contours of the antique ship and the ship number 747.

"Annie, I thought you wouldn't come."

My face flushed and I turned around, startled and embarrassed.

"I came yesterday, but you were up in the air."

"Oh." He looked surprised, as if I'd thrown out our friendship almost as fast as he did. At first his lack of confidence in me hurt, then I grew defensive. *Serves him right.*

"Listen, Mom and I dissected that flower Nova gave us, and we've found a bunch of microbes which may be responsible for making people sick."

"That's great news, Annie. I knew you'd figure it out."

"That's not all. And Mom doesn't know about this part." I leaned in closer to him and whispered, "I've seen things, strange unexplainable things, leading me to believe the real threat lies beyond the ridge."

"What do you mean?"

I shook my head, wishing I could offer him more solid evidence. "I'm not sure. The problem is I have no proof, and I can't report any of this to Lieutenant Crophaven without proof. You're the only one who will listen to me that can help. You've always believed in me, and I need you to believe in me now."

He leaned in even closer so his breath fell on my lips. "What do you want me to do?"

Intoxicated by his close proximity, I had to refocus my thoughts. "I need you to detour your mission and take some aerial photos of what's behind that ridge. It could be nothing, or it could be something that poses a threat."

Sirius backed away and crossed his arms, looking around him and then back at me. "You're asking a lot. To go against my orders and change the coordinates of the mission…"

"You're the only hope I have of knowing what's behind the ridge."

"I could lose my aviator's license and everything I've worked for."

"I know." I took a deep breath, summoning the courage to ask him one more time. "Do it for the colony."

"No." His eyes creased, and I thought he'd deny me and we'd all die a horrible death from microbes infecting our bodies, like the aliens before us. I moved to turn away, but his hand held my arm and he leaned in close again. "I'll do it for you."

Before I knew it, he leaned toward me and his lips touched mine. Warmth flowed from my mouth all the way down to the bottom of my stomach. So many times I dreamed of this moment, but never under these circumstances. Part of the kiss felt so undeniably right, and another part felt heartbreakingly wrong. I ignored that part and kissed him back for a second, reveling in the softness of his lips. Then I tore myself away and ran without looking back.

I hobbled away from the airstrip, running from Sirius, and mostly running from the truth.

He isn't mine.

I hit the jungle and sobbed, tearing the vines from the canopy as they got in my way. Sap ran down my arms as I reached the first outcropping of crystal and pounded my fists into it until it cut my arms and my blood mingled with that of the jungle's. I coughed, unable to sob any longer, and collapsed on the turf with my head between my knees.

"Bad day?"

I looked up. Ray, exactly as he was when I last left him, stood above me like an angel of light. In any other circumstance I'd be flabbergasted, but right now I wanted more than anything to be alone. "You could say that, yes." Instant guilt zapped through me. No matter what had happened to me, Ray had had the worst day of them all. "Why didn't you tell me you were dead?"

"I thought it would scare you away. Or you wouldn't believe me."

I sniffed and wiped my face on my arm. "You're probably right."

"About which one?"

I threw a vine across the jungle floor. "Take your pick."

Ray crossed his arms. "You don't have to be testy."

I scanned the jungle around us. "Where are the aliens? Why did they send you?"

Ray looked around him as if they'd appear over his shoulder. "They didn't send me. I sent myself. Besides, the whole communication thing works better if you speak the same language."

"Right." I didn't want to admit how much they freaked me out.

"Did you send someone to look over the ridge?"

I huffed, wanting to block the memory in my mind and relive it over and over again at the same time. "Yeah, he's going on the mission later today. That's *if* he takes my advice."

Ray let out a breath of relief, but no air moved above me, reminding me he wasn't really there. "Let's hope it's not too late."

"Too late for what?"

Ray shook his head. "I'm not really sure. All I know is I'm being pulled in another direction. I can't stay around here forever."

"You can't stay and help?"

"You're the one, Annie."

My eyes shot up. That's what Great-grandma Tiff used to say. The light dimmed above us and he seemed less substantial, as if the sun's rays powered the crystal, keeping his vision strong.

Suddenly I didn't want him to leave. I had so many more questions, and I didn't want to be alone. "Ray?"

"At least you had a chance to find love."

My head fell, and I stared at the vines on the ground. Was love the intense yearning that blossomed deep down in my gut? If so, I wasn't sure I wanted it. Besides, what good was love if you couldn't act upon it?

When I looked up again, he'd disappeared.

***

After Ray disappeared, I picked myself up and decided to move on with my life. How could I be *the one*? The one to do what, exactly? His last words dropped a heavy guilt on me. I wasted time brooding about what could never be when I should have been working hard to help those around me, find a cure for Amber. I stomped over the turf to the greenhouses.

Mom looked up from her experiments with shock. "Andromeda, I didn't expect you to come in today."

After how I acted last night, I wouldn't have either. "I'm sorry I've been so weird these past few days."

Mom stood up and opened her arms. "It's all right, honey. This has been a big change for all of us. I'm sorry I broke the news to you about Ray in the way I did."

I walked the distance to her and fell into her arms. I didn't remember the last time I'd hugged her and it felt good, almost as if we were a normal family again. The homey scent of her vegetable soup mingled with the lavender soap we used filled my lungs. Another scent hid among the rest—the tang of strange lab chemicals. Crystal dust coated the front of her lab coat. As I hugged her, my eyes strayed to the tables behind her and my heart flipped in my chest.

"Mom, what are you doing?"

A bed of blood-red flowers grew cased in glass in a horrific, twisted garden in the middle of the lab samples. There must have been twenty blossoms, all flourishing in the greenhouse's filtered light.

"I found some seeds in the sample Nova brought us. I'm using the accelerated growth crystals to study its life cycle."

I wanted to hold my breath and never let it go. "What if it gets loose in the air?"

Mom's lips stretched thin. "It won't. The glass is airtight. We can observe the plant throughout every form of its life cycle and perhaps locate more of them around us in the jungle turf."

The idea was brilliant, yet it made me want to quarantine the lab and shut it down, plowing the site over with a Landrover. "Lieutenant Crophaven would never authorize this."

Mom put her hands on her hips. "No, he wouldn't, but that's why he's chief of operations and I'm the microbiologist."

Mom made me proud. I was the one with space pirate in my blood, and here she was performing an illegal experiment right under the lieutenant's nose. At least someone was doing something about the problem. I stepped over to the glass and gawked at the beautiful, deadly blossoms.

"Now what are we going to do?"

Mom leaned over my shoulder to peer into the glass beside me. Her voice was hushed. "We wait and see."

CHAPTER SEVENTEEN

TRYOUTS

Laser fire erupted from the beach as I exited the *New Dawn* to start another grueling day in the greenhouses. I ran from the dock, my boots thumping on the hollow metal, and jumped to the crystals below, forgetting about my bad ankle.

People crowded along the jungle line. Had someone else besides me finally seen the aliens? My heart jumped up to my throat as I reached the edge and pushed through the gathering throng.

The man in front of me whispered, "Do you think he'll make it?"

His companion shrugged, and I slid in between them, for once glad I didn't have Nova's curves. Wiggling my way to the front, I heard someone utter, "I'm placing my bet on Corvus Holmes."

No. My body jolted and shock stole my breath away. *Not Corvus.*

Three men stood in a row, their lasers raised to the jungle. A Trisilium Bi-what's-its-name spewed tentacles in front of them, vomiting sticky, slithering tongues over the crystal beach. The appendages writhed, searching for a suction hold.

131

Lieutenant Crophaven addressed the crowd. "Each applicant will have three minutes to show what he's got. From target practice, Denneth is in the lead, followed by Corvus, and in last place, Astral."

"What's going on?" I whispered, tugging on the sleeve of the woman next to me.

"Tryouts," she answered without taking her eyes off the flower.

"For what?"

"Head of security." She finally looked me in the eye. "Ray Simmons' old job."

"Oh." I was sorry I asked. For a second, my eyes traveled the length of the jungle, expecting his ghost to be standing by, watching to see who filled his boots. Only vines cluttered the jungle. Maybe Ray had passed on, and I said a silent *thank you* to the jungle for his help.

Crophaven raised his hand and slashed the air with his arm, blowing a whistle. The men dropped their lasers and circled around it.

Anxiety clutched my insides and I could barely speak. "Why aren't they firing?"

"Can't use lasers on this part of the test."

What the hell could they use? Their bare hands?

Corvus took the first step forward, his boot stepping within centimeters of one of the tentacles.

Before I could stop myself, my voice screeched out of my throat. "Corvus, be careful!"

Even though everyone was shouting, he turned as if he could discern my voice from the throng. My eyes met his, and he smiled before he turned back to the man-eating flower.

"Couldn't they just choose someone?" I pleaded to no one in particular. Astral had sneaked up behind the flower, and a tentacle swooped though the air at his head. He ducked and jumped back.

"Head of security's a tough job." The woman raised

her eyebrow. "Crophaven wants someone who's not afraid of this planet."

Somehow I knew deep down Corvus was the right man for the job. His quiet calm made me feel safe. Nothing on Paradise 21 seemed to faze him, and secretly I wished more than anything he'd win.

Denneth grabbed a tentacle with his bare hands and pulled. The muscles in his arms bulged as the flower fought back. His boots skidded on the crystal as the tentacle pulled him closer to the stigma in the middle.

"Let go!" someone in the crowd shouted.

Denneth tried, but his hand stuck to the suction cups. He whipped the tentacle back and forth, trying to free himself, but it only drew him in further.

"Crophaven's just going to let him die?"

The woman looked at me as if I didn't know anything. I scowled back. It wasn't my fault I hadn't come early enough to hear the rules.

"No, they'll cut him out if he ends up in its belly. I heard the process takes over an hour, and he'll have acid burns on his skin."

The thought of acid burning Corvus's now very tan skin made me cringe inside. I bit my nails, deciding I couldn't watch any longer, but I couldn't tear my eyes away.

Corvus approached the flower swiftly. He ducked out of the way of the first few tentacles, but as he grew closer, a tentacle wrapped around his bicep and another around his calf.

What was he doing? People yelled at him from the crowd, and I joined in. He ignored our warnings and stepped forward. It was suicide.

My heart ceased to beat. Or at least that's what it felt like: a dead wad of flesh in my chest.

Tentacle after tentacle wrapped around Corvus until he had only one free arm. As the flower drew him in, he lunged in further. His free hand grabbed the stigma and he yanked on the end, pulling it right out of the center. The flower deflated, petals withering on the crystal beach. He shrugged off all the tentacles as if they were ribbons and turned to face the crowd, yellow stigma dangling from his hand.

Cheers filled the air and I breathed in relief. He'd won, yet I was more concerned for his well-being than any accolades. I rushed toward him, but everyone pressed in, pushing me back. Men picked him up on their shoulders and paraded him around the beach.

My locator beeped and I looked down to see a message from Mom.

There's been a change in the specimen. Come quickly.

Why now? I wanted to congratulate Corvus more than anything at that moment. Looking back once over my shoulder, I headed in the direction of the greenhouses.

CHAPTER EIGHTEEN

FREQUENCIES

I rushed into the greenhouse and Mom caught me with her arm.

"Andromeda, put your mask on."

Her tone of voice was so serious, I did a double-take to make sure she was all right. Her eyes were full of fear.

"We can't waste time."

I snapped on my mask and approached the glass case with the specimens we'd grown from the first red flower. The samples in the lab had thrived until the pods in the center turned from yellow to black-purple and swelled with squiggling microbes. When I looked inside the glass, a mucus-like substance clung to the sides, dripping and oozing, reminding me of a nasty sneeze. Pieces of torn membrane lay in the center of the red petals where the pod had been. I took in a tentative breath, reminding myself the glass separated the microbes from my lungs.

"That's the answer." Mom secured her mask before walking to the case. She shoved her hands through two plastic gloves attached to the inside to collect a sample. "They release the microbes through the air."

Just as she scooped up a spoonful of the goo, another pod burst open, splattering all over her gloves. The sound was sharp as an antique rifle shot, or the popping of a giant balloon. Mom flinched, despite the fact the glass separated her from the deadly substance.

"Mom, be careful!"

"I'm fine." She didn't look fine. Her gloved hands shook inside the glass container as she tried to steady the specimen sample to place it on a lab tray.

"These microbes can dig their way through almost anything. If they splattered in our faces, I'm not even sure the masks we have on would hold them off."

"No wonder Ray and Amber got sick." My imagination went wild with the thought of Sirius flying over exploding red flowers. Could they dig through the hull?

I thought about how long it would take him to reach the ridge, and if he'd wait until they'd accomplished the primary mission. Maybe I could get a message across to him in time to warn him.

"Any luck finding a strain of antibiotics that can kill them?" I watched her smear the sample on the lab tray and take a look underneath the microscope.

Mom furrowed her brow. "At this point, I can only stunt their growth."

Even that was impressive. I never thought a microbiologist could save lives. It made me want to reach her rank someday, to help people. "What does it look like?"

"There are microbes all over this sample. Now if only I could find a cure for Amber."

Amber. I'd forgotten about her in the thick cloud of melancholy from Ray's death. "How's she doing?"

Mom sighed as if the weight of the planet rested on her shoulders. It just might. "Her body is full of them. I've managed to keep their population from growing, but I can't seem to wipe them all out. At least they haven't infected her brain."

I swallowed a lump in my throat and forced the question out. "Is that what happened to Ray?"

Mom slid her hands out of the gloves and washed them with antibacterial soap. "I didn't want to talk about Ray because I upset you too much last time, but yes. Ray's infection traveled to his brain. His antibodies flooded around the microbes and his brain swelled. That's how he died."

I tried not to think of those little buggers eating his brain, but the image just kept sticking in my head, their pincher jaws hacking away at the pink tissue. I shivered.

"Andromeda, are you all right?"

"I'm fine." Just like how Mom was *fine*. My insides squirmed like a thousand microbes squiggled around in my belly and I needed to breathe fresh air. Not the reek of Paradise 21, but clean recycled air from the ship. I sniffed it greedily every time I passed through the threshold.

"Maybe you should take the rest of the day off." Mom wiped her hands on a towel.

I didn't want Mom to think I was weak, but I also wanted to get a message to Sirius as fast as I could. Weighing the options, I chose Sirius over my pride. "Yeah, you're right."

I picked up my backpack and walked to the portal.

"I'll be home in time for dinner," Mom offered, returning to her precious crystals, laid out on the table like jewels.

"Okay, I'll start the congealizer."

"Good, honey."

I could have said I'd jump off a cliff and she wouldn't have noticed. I'd already lost her to her experiments again, and I slipped out the portal without another word. On the way back to the *New Dawn*, I punched in Sirius's locator code with shaky fingers. I cringed at the thought of him flying haphazardly as he glanced down to see my message, but it was a small risk compared to not warning him.

My locator sent the signal, and I watched as the picture of a satellite flashed on and off as the message sent. I knew it would take longer because he was farther away, but when the screen flashed the message *Error 394: unable to locate the recipient,* I started to panic. Did they turn off his message receiver while in flight? If so, how was I ever going to get ahold of him?

My eyes traveled past the jungle to the far ridge poking the murky sky. He seemed a world away. I punched in his code again, my fingers traveling over the keys in the same pattern for the thousandth time, the same way my lips moved when I recited the Pledge of the Guide. The same error code came back again.

Pulling my eyes away from the ridge, I jogged home while wracking my brain for another way to reach him. When I got back to our family unit, a message beeped on the wallscreen from the newly established Planetary Affairs Office. Though addressed to our family, it was a general message for everyone, so I almost skipped it and tried Sirius's locator again. Maybe he'd landed and turned it back on.

An inkling stirring inside me told me to watch the message. I threw down my backpack and turned on the wallscreen. Lieutenant Crophaven's face came on and he looked even sterner than usual.

"This is a formal message to clear up speculation on the whereabouts of scout ship seven-four-seven." My heart skidded and almost stopped. I pictured the numbers in my memory as my fingers traced the metal hull of the Corsair before I met Sirius, before he kissed me. 747 was his ship, I was sure of it. I fell toward the screen, hanging on every word the lieutenant said.

"At this point there is no reason to be alarmed, but we have lost contact with the crew of seven-four-seven and the whereabouts of the ship. We believe it has something to do with the crystals interfering with our communications and are working on establishing a new frequency. I repeat, there is no cause for alarm."

I looked down at my locator and realized I wasn't the only one trying to get through. What if my directions had placed him in danger? Guilt poured over me, coating me from head to toe. I had to tell Lieutenant Crophaven where I'd sent him. I had to turn us both in.

Glancing at the time, I still had three hours before Mom came home for dinner. I looked up Lieutenant Crophaven's code and punched it in my wrist. The screen flashed *Airstrip 7, Communications Tower*. Gathering my last ounce of courage, and throwing out my stinking heap of pride, I bolted out of my family unit to Airstrip 7.

Hazy plum clouds covered the sky and I wondered if they blocked Sirius's vision, keeping him from returning home. Running past the parked Corsairs, I had no idea how I'd gain access to the control tower. The guards shot me a wary look as I ran up to them, panting and wheezing like an old woman, trying to catch my breath.

"This is an emergency. I must see Lieutenant Crophaven." Ironically, besides Nova, he was the last person on Paradise 21 I wanted to talk to, and here I was begging to see him.

The guard shifted uneasily. He appeared to weigh the options. He looked younger than my father and easier to manipulate. "Lieutenant Crophaven is very busy right now. Is there anyone else that can assist you?"

"No, I have a private message for Lieutenant Crophaven."

He gave me a look saying *I doubt that*, which made me angry and annoyed. In a split-second decision, I used my connections, hoping I didn't abuse them.

"It's from Commander Barliss."

I hadn't actually spoken to my great-granddad since we'd argued about Sirius and Corvus, but the man in front of me didn't need to know that. I flashed my locator with my last name on it to reiterate my point.

The guard waved at someone inside the control tower, and a man shuffled down the stairs behind him. "Inform the lieutenant Andromeda Barliss is here to see him."

"Yes, sir." The man disappeared up the stairway and I tried not to lock eyes with the guard, lest he see through my white lie.

The guard stared at me with big desert-cow eyes, and I busied myself retying the strap on my uniform. "What's it like being the commander's great-granddaughter?"

That question haunted me everywhere I went. Yes, I had advantages, but no one looked at the expectations heaped on me or the fact my grandpapa was connected to a machine. I kicked a crystal rock across the airstrip with my shoe. "It sucks."

He chuckled. "I doubt that."

Before I could spit out a response, the man inside returned and gestured for me to follow him. "Right this way, miss."

Fear and doubt weakened my knees. *Is this really the only way to go?* I thought of Sirius out there, with no knowledge of what he was up against, and forced myself forward. He'd have to forgive me later on, if he could.

I followed the man up the stairs to a glass room at the top of the control tower. Computer screens lined the circular wall below the sight panels, and men sat in hoverchairs, spouting coordinates and listening to headphones.

Lieutenant Crophaven spoke into a communications receiver. "Yes, yes. We're doing the best we can."

I bet he was in deep with all the missing colonists' families. I could imagine Sirius's mom in a fury on his wallscreen.

Lieutenant Crophaven turned around and gestured for me to follow him to a back room where computers beeped and wires stemmed in bunches across the ceiling.

I'd stepped inside a sub-brain of the *New Dawn*.

"Hello, Andromeda. You have a private message for me?"

I nodded and a drip of sweat fell off the tip of my nose. "I know where to find the scout mission."

"You do?" Surprise and doubt flashed in his rigid features. I swear more hairs turned gray on the sides of his head.

I cleared my throat, feeling I was in a ton of trouble with no way out. "The day I visited Sirius, I told him to scout the far ridge. I think some of the poisonous plants may be over there."

He squinted his eyes, making me feel as though I was two feet tall, and I resisted the urge to cringe.

"Nonsense. First Officer Smith would never deviate from his course."

I was the mother of all tattletales. "I asked him to, sir. He said he would."

"You must be mistaken." The lieutenant waved me away. "The last coordinates of the ship were fifty kilometers in the opposite direction."

"You have to send search teams over the ridge."

He scratched his head and looked away, as if searching for a way out of our conversation. "I thank you for your information, but we have exact coordinates to dispatch the search and rescue teams." He gave me that don't-tell-me-how-to-do-my-job look.

I had to keep trying, so I stared back at him. "I know Sirius planned to fly over the ridge."

"The idea of a first officer deviating from orders is preposterous, especially navigating into dangerous winds above the ridge. He'd have to lose his mind before he flew there. Now, I have a lot of work to get back to. So if you'll excuse me."

He pushed past me like I was a fly on the wall.

"Bradly, please show this young lady out."

"Yes, sir."

The man who brought me up took my arm to lead me back down. I wanted to yell over my shoulder, telling Lieutenant Crophaven he was wrong, but it was pointless.

As Bradly escorted me down the stairs, my mind swirled with the new information. I hadn't known about the dangerous flight winds above the ridge. Would Sirius really endanger the mission because of me? Had he crashed over the ridge where no one would find him? I knew Sirius better than Lieutenant Crophaven, and I believed he would follow my advice. He always acted like he was invincible. Nothing ever got in his way, until now.

CHAPTER NINETEEN

SHIFTING GEARS

The floor chugged underneath my feet. At first I thought I was back in space, coasting along on the New Dawn *like I had the past seventeen years of my life. My heart exploded with elation. Maybe it had all been a bad dream and Great-grandma Tiff would be waiting for me in our family unit, wanting to tell me Sirius stood at the portal to take me on another adventure.*

The floor pitched down and sprang back up again, shattering my delusion. No, I wasn't on the New Dawn. *This vessel coursed faster and lighter through buoyant air, not space. I was on a ship, a Corsair.*

Straightening up, I looked around me. Nova sat belted in a passenger's seat along with Alcor Dunstable and Lyra Bryan. I cringed at the thought of being there in my sleep-pod nightdress, but no one seemed to see me or offer help as the ship pitched again, and I stumbled into the chrome wall.

A familiar voice rang out on the intercom. "We're experiencing some turbulence due to high-speed winds. Stay seated and don't panic."

Sirius! *My whole body flipped to attention. Had I been assigned to the scout mission? Fog clouded my mind, and I couldn't remember. A strange feeling of displacement tingled in my limbs. The situation didn't seem right.*

Pushing that thought away, I picked myself up and held onto the railing securing the supply containers. Gravity pulled me back, but I fought against it and tugged my way up to the cockpit.

Nova spoke behind me, her snobby, high-pitched voice making my insides crawl.

"This flight time is taking too long. We should have been back to the base by now. Something's wrong." I wanted to crawl back and smack her. How dare she question Sirius's abilities?

Alcor peered out a small sight panel to his left. "I don't recognize that ridge."

"What ridge?" Nova squeaked.

A terrible sound wailed throughout the cabin, the sound of metal bending and a howling wind. Lyra screamed. All I could think of was reaching Sirius. I had to warn him about something, I just didn't remember what.

My feet lifted from the floor. I free-floated, like on the New Dawn *when the gravity rings cycled down. Below me, Nova ducked her head. Beside her, Alcor struggled to secure his mask while Lyra flailed around, totally freaking out. I reached down to calm her, but my head hit the ceiling and the world dimmed to black. I tried to open my eyelids, but they stuck to my face. Was I blind? I panicked, clawing at a hard surface above my head.*

***

The lid of my sleep pod rose up and light from my room poured in. I took a deep breath, sweaty and shivering at the same time. The safety of my room surrounded me, yet I trembled with the memory of my dream.

Was it a dream? It seemed so real.

I stepped out of my sleep pod and pulled on the undershirt of my uniform. My head hurt where I'd hit it in the dream, and I rubbed my hand over a bump in the back. How could I have hurt myself so badly in my own sleep pod?

Had I somehow transported myself into their Corsair? The thought was so ridiculous I laughed out loud. Yeah, next I'll have the ability to see through walls, and then to shoot lasers with my eyes.

There was only one way to be sure.

I sat on the floor next to the wallscreen and typed in *mission personnel corsair 747*. I hugged my shoulders while the computer searched for the information, hoping I was wrong.

The names popped up, and I recognized them one after another:

Sirius Smith, Navigator
Nova Williams, Team Expedition Leader
Alcor Dunstable, Medic
Lyra Bryan, Field Work Assistant

Before this, I hadn't checked to see who was on the mission with Sirius, so how did I know it in the dream? Had I overheard someone talking about it? Thinking back, I couldn't recall any particular conversation.

Could it have been a good guess? What were the odds I'd get the entire team right?

Dammit! I stank at statistics.

If I had seen it firsthand with my weird psychic abilities, then they were in trouble. No one except Great-grandma Tiff would believe me. I couldn't let this knowledge sit without acting on it. If something happened to them and I could have prevented it, then their deaths would be my fault. Thinking about how I'd sent Sirius over the ridge, they were my fault anyway.

I paced my room, thinking about all of the ways I couldn't possibly rescue Sirius. I couldn't fly a Corsair, trek across miles of jungle turf, or convince Lieutenant Crophaven to send reinforcements on the whimsy of a dream. None of it would work.

The Landrovers' giant tires came to mind. The night that Corvus showed me the excavation site, I passed by several of them, fueled up and ready to go. How hard was it to drive one?

Running my fingers along the smooth plastic lid of

my sleep pod as it sealed without me inside, I realized it didn't matter how hard it was. I'd have to figure it out. The Landrovers were my only option to set things right. I still couldn't reach my grandpapa, and my parents wouldn't disobey Lieutenant Crophaven outright, even though Mom studied the enemy right in our greenhouse. Rescuing Sirius was up to me. That thought scared me as much as it pumped courageous blood through my veins.

Without another thought, I slipped on my pants and velcroed my boots. Everyone was sleeping soundly in their pods. I could sneak out and steal a Landrover without my parents finding out until the morning. By then I'd be long gone.

After stuffing my backpack full of supplies, I tiptoed to the portal of our family unit and punched in the exit code. I typed a quick message to my parents, saying I was all right and had gone away to be alone. I programmed the message to appear well into the morning, giving me time to get away. Hopefully, they wouldn't be too angry.

The portal dematerialized, and I stepped into the dimly lit corridor without looking back. I listened for footsteps, but all I heard was the distant hum of the *New Dawn*'s operations as my grandpapa slept. A sense of timelessness fell over the ship, everything hanging in suspension, like a satellite in deep space. The vacant halls made my imagination run on overdrive.

What if I was the only person alive, doomed to roam a lost civilization. I wondered if the aliens died out all at once, or if a few survived to watch their colony perish.

Shivers tickled my spine, so I tried to refocus my thoughts on less scary subjects. I needed a plan to convince the guards to allow me to leave the ship in the middle of the night. I could tell them I forgot to turn on the irrigation system and all our plants would wither if I didn't get out there. Or I could say Mom was still in her lab and needed me to bring her something from our family unit. They wouldn't check her locator, would they?

As I weighed the various stories, I turned the corner to see a man in uniform slumped over by the exit. I froze in my tracks, thinking he was sick with the microbes. If so, I had to alert the entire ship, and then I wouldn't get five feet from the ship's portal.

He took in a deep breath and let out the nastiest snore, snot clogging his nose. I sighed with relief. He wasn't sick at all. He slept on duty! I crept up to him and felt around his neck for his ID card. If he guarded the portal, he'd have access to the outside in case of an emergency.

I found the cord underneath the fold of his uniform and slipped out the card. Ted Barrister, it read. *Well, Ted, you're going to have to explain this one to Crophaven on your own.* He shifted from one elbow to the other, but didn't wake up.

I slid his card through the portal lock, hoping it wouldn't make too loud a beep. The portal dematerialized and the humid air of Paradise 21 wafted in.

Before I entered the dark night, I clicked my locator, ejecting the energy cell. The movement was almost automatic. I'd done it hundreds of times before while sneaking around on adventures with Sirius. This time, not having it on could be dangerous. I stored the cell in my pocket. Best to keep it with me just in case.

I ran between half-constructed buildings and through metal frames for large skyscrapers to the excavation site out back. The heaps of dug-up turf lay behind the greenhouses where I spent most of my time, at the far edge of the colony where no one wandered or asked questions. Sliding down the private incline where Corvus had taken me, I trespassed into another world.

The construction team had unearthed half of the alien structures, right down to where the foundation melded seamlessly with the purple crystal in the planet's core.

I stared at exquisite architecture, impossible by our standards. Yet the towers still stood after centuries, thin pinpricks of twisting ivory, like houses of angels with numerous windows yet no doors. Geometrical patterns so intricate I couldn't tell where they started or ended were carved into the sides in a language I'd probably never understand.

Ladders were set up to reach the inside, tempting me to explore. But I had a mission to accomplish. Tearing myself away from the forgotten city, I approached the Landrovers in the back.

I had to climb the tires to reach the door. My backpack weighed me down, and I thought I'd topple over into the rotting turf they'd dug up the previous day. The stench tickled my nose, threatening a sneeze. I held my breath and squeezed the inside of my nostrils shut. My fingers found the grooves at the top of the tires and I pulled myself up.

The hatch rose with a gentle buzzing sound. Inside were two front seats and a panel of computer screens, all showing different gauges and charts. I threw my backpack into the passenger's seat and climbed into the driver's seat. Peering out the sight panel at the tangle of jungle, I touched the steering wheel. My fingers stretched around the thick plastic and I felt like a little kid in an adult's job. I tried to turn the wheel right and left but nothing happened. The Landrover must be locked down.

I pressed a few buttons, waiting for something to happen, but the most I got was an overhead light.

"Damn."

I smacked the wheel, making my hand tingle. I didn't have time for this.

"Touch the start screen."

I jumped at the familiar voice, feeling I'd been caught red-handed.

Corvus stood below me, shining a beacon light into

the Landrover.

I squinted against the light and held my hand over my eyes. "What are you doing here?"

He chuckled. "I should be asking you that."

It dawned on me as I recognized the badge on his uniform. "You made head of security?"

Corvus smiled as if he'd won the position of lieutenant. "Yes."

"Congratulations. I watched you defeat that big flower." It was a giant promotion from construction grunt to head of security, and my words weren't enough. I wished I could have been there with him in the moment, and what I offered was too little too late.

He didn't seem to mind. "I know you were there. You helped me win." He looked down, blood rushing to his cheeks.

"Me? All I did was stand there and worry. But I knew you could do it. You're the right man for the job."

"Thanks. That means a lot."

I felt my cheeks heating and I couldn't believe my reaction. It was just Corvus, but now he was different. His confidence shone stronger and it made him look older. His body filled out the uniform well. I had to remind myself not to stare. "I've been wanting to tell you, it's just I haven't had a chance."

"That's okay. I haven't been around much, and I'm sorry. It's tough adjusting to my new schedule. They need all the guards they can get to patrol, and it's my job to train them. The ones we have are overworked and exhausted. Our territory is expanding each day."

I thought of the guard sleeping at the *New Dawn*'s portal. "I guess you're right."

His tone changed from trivial to serious. "Where are you going?"

I sighed, trying to find a way out of telling him the truth, but I couldn't bring myself to lie to him. "I'm going after the missing Corsair."

"Because Sirius is on it?"

"No." My voice came out too forceful, embarrassing me. "Because it's my fault they're lost, and I know where they are."

"How can you know?"

It all came pouring out. "I have a strange feeling something bad is behind that ridge, something threatening our entire colony, the same thing that made Ray and Amber sick. I can't tell you how I know. I just know."

I ran my fingers through my hair, trying to sort it all out and explain it in a way he'd understand. "I asked Sirius to detour his scout mission to investigate the ridge. I wasn't aware of the dangerous air currents at the time. If Sirius knew, he didn't tell me. I sent him straight into danger."

His voice softened. "Annie, it's not your fault. Sirius had to make the ultimate decision to go, whether you asked him to or not."

I didn't tell Corvus about Sirius's feelings for me. I didn't tell him about the kiss. "Please, Corvus. Please don't turn me in." He'd have to risk his job for me, and all I'd ever done was brush him off.

Corvus smiled. "I'm not going to turn you in."

I blinked in shock. "It's your job."

He climbed up the tires faster than I could have taken a breath to deny him. His face came up beside mine, set in determination. "I'm going with you."

Corvus go with me to save Sirius? The irony of that situation made me want to laugh hysterically until I cried. "I'm not going to have you sacrifice your promotion for me."

"What's the use of a promotion if the colony doesn't succeed? If people die?"

My face flushed hot. Corvus believed in me as much as Great-grandma Tiff. He didn't question my feelings or my irrational concerns.

He just believed me.

I wanted to wrap my arms around him. He was so solid and sure.

Instead, I slipped into the passenger seat. "You know how to drive one of these things?"

"Of course. I used to be on the construction team, remember?"

He flicked his fingertips over a panel and slipped his ID card into a slit near the steering wheel. The computer screens came alive, lighting up the inside of the Landrover in white light.

Suddenly, being a former construction worker seemed out-of-this-galaxy cool. I smiled as big as my mouth would stretch. Corvus smiled back with a sparkle in his eyes. He shifted into first gear and the engines revved up.

"Where to?"

CHAPTER TWENTY

UNCHARTED PATHS

The world went by in a blur of green and violet in the headlights of the Landrover as we plowed our way through the jungle turf. I laughed and hollered, batting my fist in the air. Leaving the ship behind, freedom coursed through me. Corvus laughed with me, keeping his eyes on the topography charts and the path ahead of us.

Monster Trillium blossoms splattered on the windshield, spreading violet goop. Corvus clicked a switch and plastic blades swiped the vegetation off. I decided these Landrovers were the coolest invention the engineering team made. I was done with feeling sorry for Paradise 21.

"Won't they follow our tracks?"

"Nah. The scout team drove Landrovers all over this area. There must be dozens of trails. It would take them days to find ours."

"How much fuel do we have?"

Corvus wiped fog off the gauge. "Enough to go to the ridge and back again."

"Good." I sat back in relief and let my body jostle with the bumps as the tires dug up the turf underneath us.

153

It felt good to be covering some ground, cleaning up the mess I made. Although, in another way, I was making my mess even bigger. "What will they do to us?"

"Don't think about that. Think about saving the colony and your friends."

His words soothed my racing heart. Corvus always knew the right way to look at the world. He didn't let little things bother him, and I found that more and more attractive. He caught me looking at him and I flicked my eyes back to the glow of the headlights. He reached across the computer panels. My heart jumped as I thought he reached for me, but his fingers punched in a code. Light techno music drifted up from the speakers behind us. I recognized the song instantly.

He looked at me. "Do you remember?"

I did, but for some unexplainable reason I didn't want him to know. "What do you mean?"

"That's the song they played at the celebration. You know, under the light show."

Of course I knew. I couldn't hide it any longer. My face burned. "That's the song we danced to together."

"It's our song, Annie."

His words left me speechless. I'd never had something to share as a couple and I kind of liked the idea. In another way, it scared me worse than plummeting through a black hole. Both led to uncharted paths, places I'd never been before and wasn't sure I wanted to go. Here we were, driving on our own undiscovered trail. It was happening right before my eyes, and I was helpless to stop it.

Not wanting to talk about our relationship, I put my head back against the seat and closed my eyes. The rhythmic beat of the song carried me away, and I slept unhindered by dreams.

***

Hazy purple light danced in my eyes, and I wondered

where I was. I'd programmed my sleep pod to shine bright white radiance in the morning to wake me. This was nothing like it.

"Good morning, sleepy."

My whole body jerked up as the Landrover hit a bump and the night came flashing back with snippets of the techno melody. I'd escaped from the ship and stolen a Landrover. "Corvus! You drove through the whole night?"

He shrugged. "I'm used to being up all night because of my job, remember?"

Embarrassment came over me. I was the one who started the mission, yet Corvus had done all the work so far.

"I can't believe I let myself sleep so long." I looked up at the light filtering down through the vines. "It must be almost noon."

"You looked exhausted, so I didn't want to wake you."

He was one to talk. His eyes were bloodshot, and his shoulders slouched back against the seat. "You need to rest. Let me take the wheel."

He raised his pale eyebrows. "Do you know how to drive?"

I shrugged. "How hard can it be?"

"I'll have to teach you."

"I'm sure I can do it." It was the only way to keep going. Every second, Sirius and the other members of the team might be hurt or in trouble, and the pressing tick of time suffocated me.

"All right." Corvus said it as though I said I'd play a game with him. He pressed on a few pedals with his feet and the Landrover ground to a halt.

"Hold on." I unbuckled my seat restraints and rummaged through my backpack.

"Do you have Landrover operator directions in there?"

"No." I pulled out a container of dried fruit from the dehydrator. "Even better. I have breakfast."

"Wow, you came prepared." Corvus reached over and picked out a dried peach.

"Considering I had no idea how I was going to drive this thing, I don't think so." Failure weighed me down.

"I bet you would have figured it out without me." Corvus popped the peach in his mouth and took a handful of raisins.

"I don't think so." Now was the time to say it, but the words were so hard for me to form. "Thank you for driving this far."

His words flowed sweet as honey. "No problem. I'd do anything for you, Annie."

I almost choked on a dried fig. The moment hung awkward in the air between us. He drew me in like he had me on a string and twirled me closer each minute we spent together. Then I thought of Sirius lying hurt somewhere, and guilt seeped in. "So are you going to show me how to drive this thing or what?"

"Sure. Come on over."

He scooted over and I wiggled out of the passenger seat and sat in the driver's seat beside him. His body felt warm against mine as he explained the multiple screens and topography charts.

All the information made my head swirl, but I tried my best to understand.

"Watch out for the red areas on the chart. Those indicate crystals popping up from the turf and the Landrover's tires, thick as they are, can't handle their jagged outcroppings."

"Got it."

"The fuel pedal is here." He tapped the toe of his boot on the floor. I stretched my leg out but couldn't reach it.

Corvus smiled sympathetically, although I couldn't

imagine how he'd know how embarrassing it felt to be so small. "I'll adjust the seat for you."

Corvus stepped out of the vehicle and pushed the seat up so my foot could reach the pedal. He walked around the front, pulling off some tangled vines, and slipped into the passenger seat.

"Okay, navigator, give it a try."

I touched my toes to the pedal and the Landrover lurched forward faster than I thought it would. I screamed and pulled my foot off and the tires stopped abruptly, sending us both forward.

Corvus braced himself against the dashboard. "Nice try. Now, try braking more slowly."

"Shut up." I smiled, and we both laughed. Taking a deep breath, I tried again with a gentler touch. The Landrover rolled ahead, and I pressed a little harder, gaining speed. I watched the path laid out for us on the topography charts. Driving was easier than I thought.

When enough time had elapsed to convince Corvus I wasn't going to crash, he closed his eyes and fell asleep. My eyes fell into a pattern—watch the topography charts, then watch the sight panel, back and forth until the rhythm of it lulled me into a trance.

My mind roamed to places I hadn't allowed it to go before. Now and then I stole a glance at Corvus as he slept, taking in how the purple sun shined on his broad nose and how his golden blond hair, now growing out, had started to curl at the ends. Was he dreaming? If so, what were his dreams about?

What would a life with Corvus be like? He would always be there for me, no question about that. He wasn't as dumb as I'd thought he was, just subdued, not as flashy and outgoing as the others in our class. So what if he was a construction worker turned head of security? I was a species integration assistant. Together we made a well-balanced team. Why was I so against our match in the first place?

I almost forgot about the mission and Sirius. The screen beeped a warning, and I looked down to see an army of red dots approaching in a semicircle. A voice sounded: *warning, unchartable terrain.* There was no path laid out. The computer had abandoned me.

"Corvus," I shouted at him, not wanting to take my hands off the wheel. "Wake up!"

How did I stop the Landrover? I couldn't remember. I pressed every button I could and slammed my feet on the other pedals on the floor. Grasping the wheel in my slippery fingers, I reached over and shook Corvus's arm. "Wake up!"

"Huh?" He was groggy until he looked at the screens and jolted awake. "Brake, Annie, brake!"

The red dots got bigger, and the voice sounded again. *Warning, unchartable terrain.*

"I don't remember how."

"Left pedal. Push it all the way down."

I always got left and right confused. Although my schoolmates picked on me, I didn't think it was a big deal until now, until our lives depended on it.

"Left pedal!" Corvus repeated himself as if it would somehow dawn on me.

I took a guess and slammed my foot down. The crystal field grew larger in front of us like giant monster grass.

The Landrover slammed into the first outcropping, and we pitched forward. My seat restraints pushed against my chest, and for a second I thought the belts would slice me in two. I jolted backward and hit my head against the seat. Pain exploded behind my eyes. My mind jumped inside itself, blocking out the outside world.

I must have fallen unconscious because I heard Corvus's voice resonating by my ear. "You all right?"

His touch was warm against my arms and neck,

probing for broken bones. My body felt like jelly, but nothing hurt too badly. I opened my eyes and looked into his face, a breath away, so close it startled me. "Yeah. Are you okay?"

"I think so." He pulled away quicker than I wanted him to and opened his door, stepping out to assess the damage. A crystal shard pointed directly at my head, inches from the sight panel. If I'd gone any further, the tip would be staked through my heart.

"We're going to have to walk from here." Corvus didn't sound angry, but I was still embarrassed.

Galactic fail.

I wiggled out of my restraints and stepped out on wobbly legs. "I ruined it, didn't I?"

"Nah, these things are built sturdy as rocks." Corvus tapped the dented metal on the front casing. "You parked it just in time."

We both knew that was the greatest understatement of the day. Despite the circumstances, I broke out into hysterical laughter, the panic washing away.

"The Landrover can't go any farther." He winked. "We, on the other hand, can use our good old-fashioned feet."

CHAPTER TWENTY-ONE

PRIZE

The landscape glistened, reminding me of broken glass. We picked our way through the crystal field, careful not to cut our legs on the shards. Some of the surfaces were murky as frosted glass, while others showed our images clearly. Corvus came up behind me, and his blue eyes reflected a pale amethyst. I had my first glimpse of what we'd look like as a couple.

"Annie, what are you looking at?"

My face grew hot. "Nothing."

Corvus leaned in beside me and glanced down at the amethyst's surface. "Pretty, aren't they?"

I pulled away, stepping over fingers of amazonite. "Yeah, if they weren't so uber-dangerous to people driving Landrovers."

Corvus laughed. He always found me so amusing. "Still don't like Paradise 21?"

The crystals crunched under my boots. "Let's just say it's not growing on me."

"I hope it doesn't." Corvus's eyes roamed over me. "You'd look pretty silly with vines all over you. Not to mention how hard it would be to walk around."

"Ha. Ha." I faked laughter, but his goofiness lightened the mood. I tried not to worry about the absence of any signs of the ship. My emotions sank with every step we took. Maybe Sirius hadn't listened to me. Maybe Lieutenant Crophaven was right.

"The ship's not here."

Corvus shrugged. "Don't give up yet. There's still a lot of ground to cover. You did want to investigate behind the ridge, right?"

I looked warily toward the ridge towering over us. Chills ran down my back as we stepped into its shadow.

"Yeah, I'm just afraid of what we'll find."

"Better to know what we're dealing with." Corvus squinted his eyes at the ridge as if it were his enemy as well. The sky rumbled above our heads as though the heavens argued with us. Thick bruise-colored clouds moved in, churning in the wind.

"It's going to pour." He quickened his pace. "We should find shelter before we get drenched."

"Oh, yeah." I'd forgotten about the evening downpours. Thinking I'd be in the Landrover the whole trip, I hadn't brought any plastic tarps or tents to shield me—us—from the rain. I scanned the crystal field around us. I felt so naked, so vulnerable. My uniform rustled in the breeze like paper against my legs.

"Come on, Annie." Corvus tugged me ahead. "Our best chance is the ridge."

Lightning struck the sky and we ran, each step chancing a slice into our legs. The rain came next in a wave, and I stumbled forward.

"I can't see a thing."

"Hold my hand and I'll guide you."

I grasped his hand and he pulled me forward. My boots slipped on the wet crystals and I struggled to keep my balance.

"Hand me your backpack."

"I can manage." But with me hauling it around, we weren't covering much ground. As much as I wanted to hold my own, I'd have to give in this time.

I shrugged off the shoulder straps and tossed the pack to Corvus. He shouldered both his and mine and pulled us ahead. Thank the Guide one of us was built like an ox. It was much easier to balance without it.

The rain fell in relentless tides, pounding on my head and shoulders like it wanted to melt me into the turf. I fought against the pelting waves and held onto Corvus, hoping each step took me closer to someplace dry and warm. My legs ached and my hands grew so numb and wrinkled I thought they'd shrivel up.

He stopped as we approached the ridge. "There's nowhere to go."

His chest heaved, and I could tell the weight of both packs exhausted him. The rain puddled red on the crystal underneath us. "Corvus, your leg."

"Just a scrape." He collapsed on his knees. I fell beside him and examined the cut. The blood made my stomach tighten. I helped him pull the backpacks off and searched for my spare uniform shirt at the bottom. I pulled it out, and the dry cloth against my cold wet skin felt so good. I ripped off the arm and tied it around the gash in his leg as tightly as I could, wincing as I pulled the fabric against the cut. My fingers shook as I tied a knot.

"That should stop the bleeding for now." I stiffened up, sniffing rain up my nose. He'd brought us this far. He couldn't do it all alone. I blinked back tears and scanned the cliff side.

"I'm going to find shelter. I'll be right back."
Corvus's voice was weak. "Don't go alone."

"I'll be fine."

Leaving Corvus with both backpacks, I trudged forward, falling against crystals when my feet slipped on the slick surface. The rain started to puddle in between the outcroppings, and I slipped down an incline into a lake up to my chest. My arms flailed as I tried to get a grip on something and pull myself up. My water-logged boots weighted down my feet. The water moved and I screamed, thinking some sea monster reached out for me.

Something hard brushed my leg, and I scrambled up the incline, only to slip back down again. A green limb tangled around my arm. The vines! It was only vines. A particularly wide vine hung over the opposite side. I waded through the water and grabbed on, climbing up hand over hand.

My head crested the top of a hill. A strange white obelisk poked out of the crystals to my right. I pulled myself over the edge and crawled toward it. Was it a different form of crystal?

I smoothed my hand over the glistening surface, smooth and unblemished as porcelain. It reminded me of the alien towers Corvus showed me at the dig site. I stood up, taking in the circumference of something that curved, unnaturally smooth.

The hill was a spaceship.

I couldn't believe it. Why were the buildings so deep within the earth, and this spaceship right on top? My heart sped up as I wondered if some of the aliens had just crashed, but then I noticed the way the crystal had formed on top of it, bending around the structure. No, this ship had been here for a while.

No jungle turf formed on this crystal bed, so the ship, unlike the colony, was still exposed. I rounded the hull and found a crevice in the porcelain, a line stretching from the middle of the curve up to the top. Standing on my toes, I traced the line with my fingernail, reaching way up over my head.

The porcelain pulsed blue light and I stumbled back, surprised the ship would respond to my touch after being dormant for so many years. The crevice in the porcelain parted, and a hatch lifted. Stunned, I stared forever before deciding to check out what was inside. I crawled onto a smooth platform. The walls were lined with hieroglyphs: strange patterns with geometric shapes like intersecting triangles and concentric circles.

I'd had to trace the crevice to open the ship, so I figured I'd trace another pattern to get the platform to work. Holding my breath, I scratched my fingernail against a trapezoid with a circle inside it.

The platform lowered and fear sped through me as I realized I might have locked myself in the ship with Corvus still out there in the rain. The platform brought me down to a corridor with a faint pulsing light. I had no time to explore further. I wanted out of the ship so I could help Corvus.

Jumping on the platform, I scrambled to climb my way back up, but the walls were slick with no handholds. I was so far down only a sliver of light shone from the outside. The pattering of rain whispered in the distance. What had I done?

Trying not to hyperventilate, I slowed down my racing thoughts. What did I do to get down here? How did I open the ship in the first place?

The patterns looked so complex, there was no way I could figure out their strange language in a rush. Running my fingers along the walls, I found the pattern I initially traced and traced it again, risking being brought down further into the ship.

Come on, come on, come on.

The white walls responded to my touch, and the platform rose back up, taking me to the surface.
Breathing in relief, I jumped down to the crystals and took off to find Corvus. I'd left him for too long.

Where had I come from? I had to skirt around the ship and the lake, so I slogged my way back in an arc, hoping he had enough sense to stay put.

Every crystal looked the same, and I cursed myself for abandoning him. I'd brought him all the way out here and left him wounded and alone. *Some lifemate you are.* I yelled his name over and over again until my throat grew raw. I stumbled, helplessness and loneliness threatening to swallow me whole.

I remembered my locator. Jamming my hand into my pocket, I brought out the battery and stuffed it back on, waiting for a signal.

Nothing.

I stomped my boot and shook my arm, wishing it would somehow turn on. Maybe the battery had gotten too wet, or maybe the crystals interfered, but the screen remained blank.

"Damn it!" All my life I'd tried to avoid my locator, and the one time I wanted it to work, it failed. Irony laughed in my face, and I wanted to crumple and cry my eyes out.

Instead, I wandered with no clear direction. An hour passed before I saw a blur of white against the purple crystal. Corvus lay on his stomach. My heart pumped faster. "Corvus!"

I ran toward him, not caring if my legs were cut or if I fell on my face. I just wanted to make sure he was all right. Every second tore at me. When I reached him, I turned him over and cupped his face in my hands. His eyes were closed. I brought my cheek to his face and shuddered with relief when he exhaled and inhaled again.

I shook him gently. "Corvus, wake up."

He opened his eyes and smiled. Everything that had gone wrong that day dissolved.

"Annie?"

"I found us a shelter. Come on."

I hoisted him up, bracing him against me. The rain had lessened, and I could see in front of me without having to squint. The white shaft of the ship poked out from the crystals on the horizon. If I hadn't seen it up close, it would have looked like another crystal, but now I recognized the shape as something alien-made and not naturally occurring.

We made our way toward the ship, stumbling with each step. He must have weighed twice as much as me, and I struggled to support him. I knew he hated putting any of his weight on me, but every time he tried to hold his own, he wobbled. I feared he'd fall and cut something else.

"Come on, Corvus. We're almost there."

We skirted the lake and the ship came into view. Corvus looked up with wide eyes as we approached the hatch. "Holy mother of a black hole."

"You're going to have to climb up. I can't lift you."

"An alien ship? Are you sure about this, Annie?"

I shrugged. "I rode the platform down to one of the floors, and it seemed okay. At least it's dry." He paused and I laughed despite being soaked in the middle of nowhere. "The aliens are long gone. And I'm not going to try and fly it."

"I know. I'm just still trying to believe it."

I climbed up and gave him my hand. "Trust me."

He took my hand and climbed in after me. We lay together on the platform, catching our breaths. If it never rained again, I wouldn't miss it.

I sat up and found the familiar pattern of the trapezoid and the circle. "Are you ready?"

"You mean we're going down?"

I nodded. I felt tied to these strange winged creatures. They had come to me in the first place, and I wanted to know more about them. I traced the pattern, and the platform brought us down to the same corridor as before.

I helped Corvus stand and we walked into the belly of the ship, the pulsing blue light illuminating our path.

Corvus shook his head in disbelief. "How can it still

work after all these years? You'd think their energy cells would have died out."

"Don't know." I thought about how the white hull glistened in the light. "Maybe it uses solar power?"

"If it does, it's much more advanced than the *New Dawn*."

We found a room to the right and sat down on the cool floor. I dug in my backpack for the skin regenerator I'd lifted from Mom's personal tools. "Let me see your leg."

Corvus dragged his leg over to me and untied the makeshift bandage. I tried not to wince at the blood and the gash.

"I don't think a tiny laser kit can help this."

"This one's got a turbo-charged skin graph. I've seen my mom fix all kinds of cuts from the farming machinery in the biodome with this." In fact, she probably missed it as we spoke, but I didn't mention it. I swallowed back a vision of Mom's worried face and turned the laser on.

Nothing happened as the laser warmed up and the smell of blood grew thick in the air. I wondered if I'd made a mistake. Then the light brightened, forming a warm red projection on the cut. The skin thickened, forming quickly. "Does it hurt?"

"Nah, it's just warm."

When I finished, his skin didn't look quite as smooth as before. There'd probably be a scar, which would have to be taken care of in the emergency bay when we got back, but at least it stopped the bleeding.

"Does it feel better?"

"Much better. Thank you." Corvus hunched back against the crystal wall. I put the laser back, mindful to take good care of it, but my fingers fumbled with the case. It felt so strange to be in a ship that wasn't the *New Dawn*, and I wondered again what happened to them.

Corvus looked at me. "You sure these aliens aren't

going to come back and find us in their ship?"

I nodded, knowing I'd have to come clean and explain everything, even if he thought I was crazy. "I see their ghosts, Corvus."

He blinked as if he misheard me. "What do you mean?"

"I have this psychic power my great-grandmother passed down to me. Her mother before her used to tell fortunes to the space pirates on Alpha Omega. Now I have it as well. It has to do with the crystals' energy. They allow me to see ghosts. The creature I saw in the jungle was a ghost. You discovered their fossils."

"I did." He nodded, scrunching his eyebrows. "It makes sense. That's why you're the only one that's seen the aliens."

Relief spread through me as I realized he was taking me seriously. "Yup. They're trying to warn us. They keep pointing to the ridge. Something bad is over there, and I think that's what doomed their attempt at a colony."

"Wow, this is heavy stuff. I can't imagine holding all this inside. All the responsibility on your shoulders."

My insides crumbled and I felt as though I fell to pieces on the floor. Having someone else know what I was going through lifted so much weight off my shoulders. *He believed me.*

"Annie, you're shivering."

Embarrassment with my vulnerability washed over me. There was nowhere to hide from my feelings or from him.

"Come over here." Corvus raised his arm, and I settled my body against his, allowing him to wrap his arm around me and pull me close. His warmth comforted me. "We'll find out what's behind the ridge. I promise. I won't let you fail."

CHAPTER TWENTY-TWO

FLAMES

I awoke to Corvus shuffling around the room, trailing his fingers along the patterns in the walls. He still favored his leg as he moved, but at least the skin looked clean.

"Is your leg feeling better?"

"Good as new."

I stared in surprise. For someone so wary to get on the ship in the first place, he'd completely turned around. "What are you doing?"

"I think I may have found something." Corvus didn't turn around to look at me. He trailed his fingernail along a zigzag, and part of the wall separated. "Bingo!"

"Be careful." I scrambled back, expecting a bomb to go off or a booby trap to snare our legs.

Corvus smiled. "Don't worry. It's just a wallscreen, I think."

He wiped his hands across the thick layer of dust to clear the screen. Pixels blinked in and out like a million winking stars until a picture solidified. Corvus joined me on the floor. I whispered under my breath, "No way."

Lines of pale-skinned aliens stood in a circle before a great ship, larger than the one we sat in. High towers surrounded them on all sides, glistening in an oily pinkish-white sheen. A sky red as blood shone in the background, casting the horizon in a hellish glow.

Corvus whispered, as if his voice would break, "I thought a purple sky was bad."

"Something's off." I leaned forward. "There's something wrong with their sun."

Brilliant spots mottled the orb's surface and I thought back to my class in astronomy. My heart plummeted. "I think their sun is dying."

"What are they holding?" Corvus pointed to one of the alien's slender, branchlike arms.

"Is it a pod?"

"No." Corvus stood up and ran his finger along the curve. "It's an egg."

Each alien carried one to the ship, clutching the smooth oblong shape with both arms. "Do you suppose they're their children?"

Corvus shrugged. "Might be."

Then it hit me all at once. "What if Paradise 21 was their only chance?"

I tried to find another ship on the screen, but I couldn't see anything past the high towers.

Corvus took my hand and squeezed. "I'm sure they had other ships. Just like us, they wouldn't put all their hopes in one ship on one planet."

His reasoning seemed logical. Still, my heart ached for them. To come from a dying world to a new one, then to have their colony fail. It was horrible. I stood up, releasing his hand as anxiety hit me like a laser bolt. I wasn't going to let whatever happened to the aliens happen to my colony. Their warnings, and their demise, would not be for nothing.

"We have to find out what's behind that ridge." I looked at his leg. "Can you keep going?"

He bent his knee and tested, putting weight on his

calf. "I think so."

"Good." I stuffed the skin regenerator into the pack. "Let's hope it stopped raining."

We followed the corridor to the platform. I traced the pattern and we rose to the surface. Part of me wanted to stay and explore the ship, to watch more of their videos and learn more about them. But time slipped through my fingers. Sirius was still out there, along with whatever lurked behind the ridge. We had to press on.

Corvus moved slowly, and it took us the rest of the day to pick our way through the crystals to the bottom of the ridge. The wall of crystals rose up in slabs, with cylindrical conglomerations sticking out every few feet. At least we'd have handholds and places to tie our rope.

"Let's make camp." Corvus slipped off the backpacks. Even with his leg still healing, he insisted on carrying both. "I don't want to climb in the dark."

Neither did I. I wasn't even sure I could climb it in broad daylight. I swallowed down my fear. We had to find a way.

After eating some soybean wafers and dried fruit, Corvus started a fire. We sat together on a slab of crystal, watching twilight turn to darkness around us. I shivered, hugging my shoulders. My clothes were still damp from yesterday, and the temperature plummeted with the oncoming night. Corvus put his arm around me, and I snuggled against him like I had last night. I wondered if we'd make it a habit. I wouldn't admit it out loud, but I liked being in his arms.

The fire crackled and I watched the flames skip and leap.

Corvus took a deep breath. "Back on the *New Dawn*, before we landed, before I knew you, I didn't want to reach Paradise 21."

His words filled me with relief. So I wasn't the only one. I craned my head up to look into his eyes. "Really?"

"Yeah. Silly, huh?" He laughed to himself. "I wished we'd have problems with the engines, or that we'd drift off course, or have to slow down to conserve fuel—something to keep us from reaching here."

"Why?"

"I didn't want my life to change. I was lazy. It was easy for me to skip class. I used to go to the gym and relax on the viewing deck, watching the stars. I knew what to expect, you know? I knew what my life would be like the next day, and the next. Paradise 21 seemed like such a big question mark, and I knew I'd have to suck it up and start working hard." He sighed. "I never told anyone. Guess I was too embarrassed."

"You shouldn't be. I felt the same way."
Corvus pulled back to see my face. His eyes were skeptical, like I teased him.

"It's the truth. When my great-grandmother died, I fell to pieces. I knew that phase of my life was coming to a close and I didn't want to change. That's why I never studied for the tests. I lived in denial for so many years."

"Wow, Annie. I always thought you were a model student."

"Ha! Me? A model student?" Corvus hadn't known me at all. Either that or I put up a good front.

Corvus's arms tightened around me. "You know what? Now that we're here, I wouldn't be anywhere else in the universe."

I thought of my own situation. *Where did I want to be?* I'd wanted to go backward for so long, to be in that room with Tiff, hearing her stories about the space pirates. But now, I enjoyed this adventure and all the freedom that came with it. I was doing something much more important than procrastinating on my homework and sneaking around with Sirius in the biodome. It was the first time I believed I could make a difference and save the colony, like Tiff had said.

Corvus's voice pulled me back from my thoughts. "There's so much I want to tell you."

His voice was calm, yet full of emotion, and I tensed up. Did I want to hear what he had to say? Anxiety rose inside me, but I couldn't bring myself to stop him. He'd done so much for me and my feelings were growing like Mom's tomatoes. *Out. Of. Control.*

As he spoke, he ran a hand through my hair, sorting out the tangles. "When I got my lifemate assignment, I was beyond happy. I couldn't imagine a better partner. You're beautiful, smart, and friendly, but I also felt guilty and nervous, as though they handed me a prize I didn't deserve."

He sighed and shifted as if his own thoughts made him uncomfortable. "When I saw you in the corridor the day assignments were made, my heart sank. I knew you weren't happy with the results. I hadn't done well on the tests because I never took school that seriously. To tell you the truth, I just liked to relax and have fun. After seeing your face, I realized I had to make something of myself. From then on, I made it my purpose to work to deserve you. I've tried so hard, Annie. I worked hard for that promotion. I'm worried I'll never be enough in your eyes."

His speech gripped my heart and held it, revitalizing it, making it want to beat. I wanted to make everything right for him in that moment, to give him what he sought: a part of myself. I reached my head up and brought my face to his, brushing my lips up against his cheek, and then finding his mouth.

Corvus held me close and kissed me back. Unlike the kiss with Sirius, this one felt right. I delved into those emotions, embracing them for the first time.

We kissed until my mouth grew hot and numb. I fell asleep in his arms, wanting the moment to last forever.

AUBRIE DIONNE

CHAPTER TWENTY-THREE

ASCENT

The next morning I woke up to the smell of smoke and a hazy purple light.

"Hey, sleepyhead. Breakfast's ready."

For a second, I forgot where I was. Dizziness swirled through me like someone spun me around until I landed in a different place. The sky was still purple, but the light shined brighter and clearer than before. My entire purpose had changed overnight. I had everything I ever needed all along. I'd blindly chased Sirius as if I had chained myself to him, using him to define me. He wasn't who I thought he was.

All this deep thinking made my head hurt, and I stuck my face down between my arms and groaned.

"What's the matter?"

I rubbed my temples. "The more I think, the worse it gets."

I heard the clank of a cooker lid and sniffed food. Corvus must have found my stash of powdered eggs. "What do you mean?"

"Never mind."

Corvus continued, as if what I said made perfect

sense. "Anyway, I figure if we start climbing after breakfast, we can reach the top of the ridge before nightfall."

Two truths remained in the mishmash gurgling in my head. Sirius was still out there, and so was the threat to the colony. Whatever my feelings for Corvus, I still had to investigate the ridge. I picked my head up. "Really?"

"Yeah."

I wondered why Corvus was in such a hurry to get there. What did he think we'd find? I opened my mouth to ask him, but he brought a tray of scrambled eggs over and my stomach grumbled. "Thank you."

"No problem." He winked and sat next to me with his own tray.

I stuffed a forkful of the eggs into my mouth and barely chewed before swallowing them. "You're a good cook."

He shrugged. "Just followed the directions on the back of the container. Hmm…master chef. Hey, do you think they'll promote me again?"

I laughed. "I'm not sure head of chefs is any higher up than head of security."

He shrugged. "Guess you're right."

Although he tried to make light of the morning, the end of our journey weighed on my mind. "What do you think we'll find over the ridge?"

Corvus creased his pale eyebrows. "Not sure. All I know is we have to find out to get some answers. Whatever is up there, we'll deal with it together."

It hit me like the wake-up call on my sleep pod: with Corvus, I never felt alone. He stood by me despite the danger and all my talk of seeing ghosts. Sirius had other aspirations. Rising up the chain of command, being an aviator, then maybe a lieutenant. He cared about the system and what everyone else thought. Granted, he might have sacrificed that to look over the ridge. But for Corvus,

I was enough. I was his dream.

I had a lot to think about and a whole day of climbing to figure it out. I finished my eggs. "Let's do it."

Corvus took my tray and stacked it against his, shoving them both into the backpack. "Whatever you like."

The climb loomed over us, and my ankle ached from the previous day's trek. I took each step slowly, securing my footing before placing all my weight on the next level up. Corvus climbed two steps ahead of me and reached down for me whenever I needed an extra hand.

We rose above the vines of the jungle. The silver frames of our buildings poked out of the landscape like alien growth on the horizon.

My stomach flipped when I looked straight down, so I kept my eyes on the sky. The longer I climbed, the more I missed my sleep pod aboard the ship, and even my boring plant job back in the greenhouses.

The purple sun had risen to a great ripe plum in the sky before Corvus spoke. "We're almost there."

He quickened his pace as we reached the summit and pulled himself up over the ridge. He gestured for me to follow, but I waved him back. "Let me catch my breath."

While I sat and huffed, he dug in his pack and took out a pair of binoculars.

I'd stolen a Landrover, driven to the edge of existence, and climbed all the way up the ridge, and I realized I didn't want to know. My voice trembled. "What do you see?"

"Annie, you were right."

I scrambled to catch up to him and almost fell back. He caught my arm and pulled me up. The landscape below us was a blur of red. It could only be one thing.

Corvus handed me the binoculars and I peered through, struggling to keep them steady in my shaking hands. Groves and groves of the poisonous plant blanketed the valley floor. I should have realized it when Mom and I tested the specimen in the greenhouse. The pool of humid air provided the perfect seeding ground.

I gasped, then realized I'd just taken in a breath full of air above a city of squiggling microbes waiting to be released. I clutched the slim barrier of my mask with my hand as if my skin could filter the air any better.

"It's the poisonous flower that made Ray and Amber sick."

I turned to Corvus, dropping the binoculars. "How did you know what it looked like?"

"I didn't." Corvus shook his head. "I wasn't looking at the flowers."

"Then what were—"

Before I could finish my sentence, a glimmer of silver caught my eye. I raised the binoculars and focused on the spot, adjusting the range of the lens. A Corsair's wing poked through the horrific garden like a broken and discarded toy. My insides squeezed so hard I couldn't take in another breath.

Corvus put a hand on my shoulder. "Don't worry. We'll get them out."

I'm glad he didn't add *if anyone is alive in there*.

The Corsair must have gone straight down because no tracks cut into the blossoms. The hilly terrain provided no runway. The ship must have crashed. So did my heart. I'd sent him there.

Corvus kept his cool, assessing the situation. "I see a path down the ridge toward the east. We'll have no trouble getting down there. The only problem is reaching it through all the poisonous plants."

I tried to settle down and think about how long it took them to explode in the greenhouse. I picked up the binoculars and focused on the blossoms. It looked like most of them were in what Mom called phase two of the growth cycle. The pods were still forming.

"If I'm right, we have a few days before they become dangerous."

"What about our masks?"

I shrugged. "I'm not sure they'll help, but I'm keeping mine on just in case."

"Okay." Corvus tightened the straps of his. "Let's kick some plant butt."

We climbed down the incline toward the valley floor. The closer I got to the flowers, the more I wanted to hold my breath. I had to remind myself the microbes couldn't get to me until they splattered and became airborne. The faster we went in, the faster we'd get out. I plunged ahead, each step a large leap.

The stems towered over our heads, and the plants weren't even finished growing. They had another few days, which meant they could possibly rise up out of the gorge and blow down the ridge toward the colony.

"How are we going to get through?"

Corvus took out his wire cutter and hacked the first few down, making a path. I remembered the way he'd confronted the Trillium Bisonate without fear. "We'll cut our way through."

I reached in my pocket and took out the wire cutters he'd given me.

"You kept them?"

"Of course I did."

What did he expect me to do with such an expensive tool? Still, his happiness made me blush. I hacked at the first plant in my way, and it fell in a limp arc to the ground. I wished I could have cut them all to shreds, but time was against us, and we had to get to the ship and get everyone out before the pods started to explode.

It took us an hour to hack a path through. My arms dripped in plant ooze by the time we reached the ship. The Corsair had struck the ground at a side angle, gouging into the turf. I ran around the half-sunken wing to the side where the numbers were painted. There it was: 747.

"Hello!" I pounded my hands on the metal. "Is anyone in there?"

The silence stung my body and shattered my soul. I tried again. "Hello?"

A muffled banging came from inside. I squeezed my ear against the metal and heard it again, this time with what I thought might be voices.

"Corvus, I heard a noise. Someone's alive."

"Where's the door?" Corvus circled the ship.

"Oh no. It's crushed underneath the turf."

Just as I spoke, a popping sound erupted behind us, sending a sickening jolt of energy through my veins. I'd heard it once before in Mom's lab. "No, no, no."

"What is it?"

I whipped my head around, but all of the pods near us were still intact. "The plants. Some of them have blossomed early." I looked at Corvus. "What should we do?"

"Dig." He threw himself onto his knees and tore through the turf. "Hurry."

I'd never seen him move so fast. In a delayed reaction, I knelt beside him and began to pull the long strands of vines from the Corsair's belly. As we dug, another pod exploded, and another. I thought microbes squirmed all over me. I slapped at my skin, but nothing was there. I couldn't see them anyway.

"They haven't exploded near us." Corvus put a reassuring hand on my shoulder. "Keep digging."

"Okay."

The top of the hatch poked out through the turf, and I clawed at the frame. "There it is!"

Corvus spoke through clenched teeth as he dug. "It won't open until we unearth the bottom."

Turf piled up around us in heaps. I didn't think it could grow so deep into the black crystals. At least the vines had cushioned the Corsair as it went down. I couldn't imagine how the hull would have looked if it hit the sharp crystals instead.

We reached the bottom of the hatch and I had to swipe away dead flowers, my hands touching pods with microbes writhing around inside. I couldn't imagine what Mom would say. Shrugging it off, I wiped my hands on my pants and slapped the door panel.

"Stand back." Corvus pulled me away just as the hatch rose.

I held my breath. The moment hung in the air for an eternity. The only sound was the buzzing of the motors lifting the hatch.

The first face I saw was the last person I ever wanted to see. I almost stepped back and gagged.

Corvus spoke from behind me. "Nova, are you all right?"

She ignored him and stared straight at me with a mix of disgust and surprise. "You're part of the search and rescue team?"

"We've come to help." Corvus offered his hand.

Nova hesitated, then slipped her hand in his.

"Nova, we have to hurry. Is everyone else inside?"

Nova's ravishing auburn hair looked greasy and flat. "Yes. Everyone's okay, but we've been stuck for days. Lyra has a broken leg, but she'll live."

"I'll help carry her out." Corvus jumped inside, and Nova turned to me. "Where's the rest of the team?"

Was it so hard for her to believe Corvus and I could get this far on our own? "This is it. It's just us."

"What?" Her eyes flared like emeralds under firelight. "Where's the rescue ship? How are we supposed to get back?"

"We have to climb back over the ridge. There's a Landrover parked at the edge of the turf." I neglected to tell her about the state it was in. I didn't think it would improve her already nasty mood.

"Climb over the ridge?" Her face contorted so much her mask scrunched up.

"Enough complaining," Corvus yelled from the hatch. "Help me get Lyra out."

I ran to him, leaving Nova to gripe. As I stuck my head inside the ship, Sirius lifted Lyra's leg. The others put their arms underneath her body.

Sirius locked eyes with me, and I gushed with a mix of emotions.

"Annie, I can't believe you found us."

I didn't want to have this conversation with everyone around, but there was no time for it otherwise. The pods were exploding, and I didn't think we'd have the chance again. "Sirius, I'm sorry I sent you over the ridge. I didn't know about the dangerous winds."

"I'm glad you did." He waved his arm around. "Have you taken a look around? Nova says the flower she gave you matches the plants surrounding us. We've found the source. You're going to save the whole colony."

"That's if we can get out alive," Corvus interrupted Sirius's syrupy tone. "The red pods are already exploding around us, sending small microbes into the air. Put on your masks and keep them on. We have to hurry."

Lyra moaned. "It hurts to move."

"Be gentle," Alcor instructed as Corvus and Sirius brought her up out of the hatch. I noticed he had a bandage wrapped around his head. Blood stained the white cotton above his right eye. Just looking at it gave me a headache. I remembered my dream and wondered how traumatizing the crash must've been.

We slipped on our masks as Alcor pulled a fold-up stretcher out from the medic closet onboard the crashed hovercraft. He secured Lyra as best he could. Alcor and Sirius carried either side while Corvus and I led the way back through the path we'd carved out of the plant husks.

Nova trailed behind.

Popping noises followed us as we hustled through the plants. I winced, scrunching up my eyes.

Corvus took my hand and pulled me forward. "Come on."

I stumbled a few times, and each time I fell I thought I'd die right there, covered in microbes. Corvus always pulled me up. I cast my eyes ahead to see if any of the pods were swelled in stage three of the life cycle, but I realized the majority of early bloomers must have blossomed where the valley mist was the thickest, at the center. We were lucky in at least that much.

We made it to the ridge's edge and started to climb. Lyra's stretcher slowed us down, and we had to take turns grabbing a side and hauling her up.

"How tall do these plants grow?" Alcor took up the stretcher by my side.

Should I tell them the truth? I figured I owed them as much. "In another few days, they might rise up out of the valley."

He put a finger up and tested the wind. "I'm not a weather analyst or anything, but the way the wind is blowing, I'd say the entire colony is downwind of this valley. A storm's brewing on the horizon."

I looked up to where he gestured and my breath caught in my throat. Black-purple storm clouds hung in the distance. "We need to move faster." I hoisted up Lyra's stretcher and pushed forward, ignoring my aching muscles. "Now."

CHAPTER TWENTY-FOUR

RACE

"Why didn't you notify Lieutenant Crophaven of our coordinates?"

It had only been a few hours and already Nova grated on my nerves. As we crested the ridge, Corvus had taken my place holding Lyra's stretcher, leaving Nova and me to find the best way down. Not the ideal pairing, if you asked me.

"I tried to, but he ignored me." I jumped from one incline to another, then turned to glare at Nova.

She snarled. "What about the search parties?"

"They were all headed in the opposite direction." I tried to explain, but I felt as though I talked to a mis-programmed computer.

"That's because Sirius deviated from course." Nova's voice seeped with disgust. "He endangered all of our lives for a whim."

"Nova, he was right. If you haven't already noticed, an entire valley of that awful plant is behind us. It's very likely that oncoming storm will blow the microbes right down onto our colony and kill everyone."

My voice rose as I spoke, and I took a deep breath to

try to calm myself before I started to punch some sense into her.

Nova's eyes narrowed. "You asked him to scout here all on speculation. You're not even sure it will affect the colony."

"Look behind you. I think a field of those red flowers is proof enough."

"We'll see what Lieutenant Crophaven thinks." Nova stuck her nose up in the air. "I'm not going to support you on this. I was dragged along against my will, with no knowledge we defied orders, and that's how it will stay."

"Fine. You don't want to take responsibility, then you don't have to." I jumped down onto another slab.

"You don't have an excellent reputation to waste." Nova jabbed her thumb against her large breasts. "I do."

Her words stung. My reputation wasn't as good as hers, but she didn't have to stick it in my face. I stood, unable to move, as if she'd thrown a dart into my back.

"If you were so intent on seeing what was behind the ridge, you should have gone instead of asking him to do it for you." Nova spat her words out and pushed ahead of me.

"Not all of us are team expedition leaders, Nova. We're not all as successful as you. It's not easy to get here without a Corsair."

I stopped on the ledge and clutched an outcropping of crystal. Frustration and anger welled up inside me, boiling until I thought my head would explode like one of those pods. As much as I hated to admit it, she was right. I didn't need Sirius to go after the ridge. I could have done it myself. I just didn't have the nerve.

A hard coil formed inside my stomach, and I straightened up. Somewhere along the way, I'd found the strength inside myself. Now I needed it more than ever.

Nova was headed for a dead end. She hadn't come up the ridge in the first place, and so her navigational skills were only guesswork. I'd climbed this ridge and knew just where to go.

I yelled at her, "Nova, you're going the wrong way."

She froze and I pushed past her, taking up the lead.

"You're right. I should have gone myself. I'm just as capable as a stuffy-nosed team expedition leader who thinks she's better than someone who expected the commander to just dump a high position on her. Maybe you were right then, but you're not now. I'm gonna get us out of here."

Her lips formed a thin line as I turned away. Smiling to myself, I called out to the others. "Over here. It's the best way."

***

Night fell in a cold hush of lavender twilight. Every muscle in my body told me to stop while every neuron in my brain screamed to push on. We reached the bottom of the ridge, but we still had to find the Landrover and plow our way back through the jungle.

The ridge blocked any vision of the oncoming storm, but static friction sizzled in the air behind us as if Paradise 21 concocted the maelstrom to rid itself of us all.

"Can't we stop for the night?" Lyra complained. "All this bumping up and down is making me sick."

"No," I snapped. "Absolutely not."

"Annie's right." Corvus said as Alcor handed him his half of the stretcher from the last outcropping of the ridge. "We have to keep going to warn the others in time before the storm hits."

I wished again for our locators to work and checked mine. The screen remained blank, even when I ejected and reinserted the energy cell. If only we could get help and alert the colony at the same time. Life wasn't that easy. It never was.

As I slipped the locator back into my pocket, Corvus approached and whispered under his breath, "Annie, do you remember where the Landrover is?"

I scanned the horizon, trying to spot landmarks. The crystal field sprawled out before us in a monotonous prickle of shards. Panic rose inside me. What if we couldn't find it? I whipped my head around.

Focus. I can do this.

The alien ship lay behind us to the right. I traced our journey back from there. "I can find it."

He sighed in relief. "Good, because I was so out of it I can't even remember crossing much of this."

He sounded as though he'd failed me. I put my hand on his shoulder and squeezed. "You were losing blood. It's not your fault."

He pulled his mask back and smiled. I realized I missed seeing his whole face. All the stress around us melted away until it was just him and me. "I'm glad you had the strength to save me."

"I'm glad you decided to help me in the first place instead of turning me in."

"Can we get going?" Sirius yelled from behind us, sounding more annoyed. "This stretcher is getting heavier by the minute."

"Of course. We're just checking our coordinates." Corvus looked toward me.

I pointed in the direction where I'd crashed the Landrover. "This way."

Lightning cracked open the sky above our heads and an ominous current of wind blew down from the ridge, flinging back my hair.

"The storm! It's caught up to us already." Alcor's voice trembled. He dropped the stretcher and Lyra shrieked. Alcor put his hands up to his bandaged head. "We're too late."

"Shut up!" Nova's eyes seared like lasers. "You're not helping."

"We can still outrun it," Corvus reassured him.

"Once we get to the Landrover, we're all set."

"We're not getting anywhere arguing," Sirius shouted as the sky started to drizzle. "Come on."

Corvus took Alcor's place on the other side of the stretcher, and we ran faster than any of us had run before. The storm rode on our heels. Puddles formed in the chasms between crystal slabs and the terrain grew slippery. Just before I thought the crystal field would never end, vines clustered on the horizon. We neared the jungle's edge.

Doubts set in as to where we'd left the Landrover. What if my estimation was wrong? The entire team relied on my poor memory, and I couldn't let them down. I charged ahead in the lead, trying to recognize any of the crystal conglomerations. Every shard looked the same.

A gut instinct told me to sway right, and so I plunged ahead, calling out behind me, "Over here."

The large crystal shard that had almost impaled me rose up above my head, pointing to the Landrover's dashboard. Relief flooded my veins until I felt like I'd melt into a puddle. I'd found it. I almost kissed the hull with my lips.

Nova climbed through the last of the crystals. "We're riding back in that?"

I pulled myself back together. "What did you expect? A shiny new Corsair?"

"It's all wrecked up," she spat out.

I used the most reassuring voice I could muster. "It'll work."

As the others caught up to us, I opened the hatch and climbed into the driver's seat. Corvus had left his ID card in the main panel, so I touched the start screen and the interior lights flashed on. Sirius and Corvus loaded Lyra's stretcher and everyone climbed in. Sirius took the seat beside me, surprising me. I looked back at Corvus, but he tended to Lyra, wiping rain off her face.

"You know how to drive this thing?" Sirius's eyes widened with a new level of respect.

"Corvus taught me."

His voice hardened into a growl. "I see."

Rain hit the dashboard in a sheet. I turned on the wiper blades, and a sticky substance formed on the tips.

"What is that?" Nova lunged from the backseat, sticking her head between Sirius and me.

I knew exactly what it was, but my heart didn't want to accept it. "It's the microbes! We have to move."

I pulled a lever and the Landrover lurched in reverse. I turned the steering wheel and we collided into the jungle. My brain worked overtime as I plowed through the vines at maximum speed and scoured the topography charts.

"How long will it take us to get back?" Alcor's voice still trembled.

"I don't know." I tried to calculate how long it took us in the first place while driving at the same time.

"Twelve hours," Corvus answered for me. "That's if Annie can maintain this speed."

"I'll try. Everyone check your locators to see if they work. Once we clear the crystals, we should get a stronger signal. That way we can alert the colony before the storm reaches them."

"What about us?" Alcor was having a mental breakdown right in the backseat and it made me even more nervous than driving under a poisonous rain while trying to navigate through uncharted terrain.

"Annie can out-speed the storm." Corvus made it sound like I was a god. "She'll get us out of this in time."

Nova's scoffing haunted me from the backseat. "We'll see."

CHAPTER TWENTY-FIVE

LADDERS

I drove forever and then kept going. My eyelids twitched and my hands hurt from squeezing the wheel, but I pressed on, flicking my gaze between the charts and the dashboard. The rain stopped, and I drove out from under the fingers of the storm. Although microbe-ooze no longer clung to the windshield, we'd have hours at most to evacuate the entire colony. I glanced down at my locator, but the device lay dead in my lap.

I thought everyone around me had fallen asleep until I heard Sirius murmur beside me.

"Annie, you've changed so much."

"Not really." I shrugged it off, feeling awkward. At least I had an excuse to keep my eyes on the path ahead. "I'm still the same girl you grew up with."

"Really?"

The way he said it made me realize I wasn't the same girl at all. I had grown in so many ways, and during the process I'd left him behind. He'd always led me ahead as if I had no direction, and I hadn't.

My life had direction now, and I realized he wasn't in it. Before I could respond, he slid next to me, so close our legs touched, and whispered, "You're stronger now, more sure of yourself. You've done so much for the colony. You're a hero."

A few days ago I would have given anything to impress him. Now his intensity made me squirm. There was something fundamentally wrong about his attention. Why didn't he like the old Annie?

"Sirius, I'm trying to drive."

"Of course." He backed away and leaned against the door. "You know, I've been thinking about the assignments. You were right. We should have gone to your great-grandfather and put in a request."

My world had changed so much since that awful day in the corridor outside his family unit. He finally spoke the words I wanted to hear, but now I worried more about Corvus. What would he say if he knew I'd talked to Sirius about changing the assignments? We had created something so perfect, so beautiful, and I didn't want Sirius ruining it.

I stole a look in the rearview mirror, but Corvus's eyes were still closed. Alcor snored, Lyra lay motionless on her stretcher, and Nova curled up against the door frame.

"Nova hates me!" His whisper hissed across the dashboard, and I looked back to make sure he hadn't woken Corvus.

"Shh!"

"She hates me," he repeated, but this time softer. "I tried to get to know her. I really did. She thinks she's too good for me, and now that I deviated from the mission, she won't even talk to me."

"I see." I held my nose up. "So I'm your second choice."

He wiped his face with both hands. "No, Annie. You've got it all wrong. I was just trying to follow the Guide, to do the right thing. I realize now, it's always been you."

Too bad it was too late. No matter how sincere his

words sounded, I felt like a second choice, only good enough for him when I'd saved the colony and when beautiful Nova said no. Corvus had always stood by me, and I wasn't about to jeopardize our relationship to give my heart back to Mr. Fickle.

"I no longer feel that way."

Sirius leaned back. I glanced over to see shock etched on his face. "You don't mean that."

"I'm meant to be with Corvus. He's done so much for me, and he never gave up on us. The more time I spend with him, the more time I want to spend with him."

Sirius looked like he'd swallowed poison as he turned away from me. I'd broken the bond we had, and it was irreversible. I wanted to say something to comfort him, but anger edged my tongue and everything I thought of would make the situation worse.

A beep sounded from my lap, breaking the silence. The sound of clothing ruffled behind me as people stirred and woke.

"Shut off the alarm," Lyra whined. "Just a few more minutes of sleep."

"Lyra, we're not on the *New Dawn*, remember?" Nova sounded annoyed.

"What's that noise?" Alcor rubbed his eyes.

My heart quickened. The Landrover shuddered underneath me and the wheels ground to a halt.

"What's wrong?" I pushed the pedal harder with my foot, but nothing happened.

"Did she break it?" Nova was always the supportive one.

"No." Corvus stuck his head over my shoulder to read the gauges. "It's beeping because it's out of fuel."

"What?" Alcor screeched.

"Stay calm and let me think." Corvus peered out the windshield. "We're got to be close. We could walk the rest of the way."

"I'm not going out there with that storm coming." Nova sat back in her seat. "We're better off in here."

Alcor's voice rose. "With no food or water left? We could be stuck here for days."

"I'd rather be stuck here and starve than have those microbes eat my brain." Nova crossed her arms.

Corvus sighed. "I'm not leaving anyone behind."

Meanwhile, the storm loomed closer. My fingers still clutched the wheel, and I pried them off. "We have to decide on something!"

While they argued in the back seat, Corvus dug in the rear of the Landrover. I wondered what he searched for that could possibly help us? Food, water, steel masks?

"Flares!" Alcor clapped Corvus on the back. "Genius."

"Not really." Corvus lifted the back hatch of the Landrover. "Just practical."

I wanted to yell at him to stay under cover, but someone had to risk the rain to alert the colony and get us rescued. I just didn't want it to be him. "No, wait. I'll do it."

"Stay inside, Annie." Corvus sounded determined.

"He's right," Nova scolded me. "Corvus is much taller and has a better chance of firing it above the canopy."

I fumed in my seat. Nova was pretty tall. Why couldn't she go out?

She's not as tall as Corvus. I turned around and crossed my arms, slumping back into the seat. The sooner he got out there, the sooner he'd be able to come back in. "Fine."

"If the storm reaches us, don't come out and get me." His words slashed my heart. I wanted to tell him I wanted him instead of Sirius right then, but some stupid fear of revealing my feelings in front of everyone held me back.

Corvus jumped out. We heard his footsteps on top of our heads as he climbed the vehicle. I watched through the dashboard sight panel, each moment squeezing more air out of my lungs. I regretted asking Sirius to change the assignments without even giving Corvus a chance, but mostly I regretted being a coward and not telling Corvus how I felt about him.

We heard three shots. The vines moved in the wind and the approaching storm brewed anxiety in my chest. "Come on, Corvus," I whispered. "You've fired the shots, now come back down."

Corvus's boots clunked on the ceiling. He jumped off, and grunted as he hit the ground. I waited for the hatch to lift, but nothing happened. *Frickin' quasars! What is he doing?*

I knew him by now. If he'd gotten infected, he wouldn't come back inside. My heart thumped so hard it hurt. I couldn't imagine going back to the ship without him, leaving him out in the jungle as he got sick. *I want to stay with him.*

The hatch lifted, and my body collapsed with relief. Corvus climbed back inside. His cheeks were flushed with exertion as he slipped back into his seat. "Let's hope they saw it."

***

The jungle vines moved above us, and I wondered if the storm had finally caught up. I stuck my face all the way up to the top of the windshield. Rope ladders fell through the canopy.

My voice rose above all the commotion. "They've found us!"

We piled out of the Landrover just as men in bio-suits climbed down the ladders. Three Corsairs hovered over us. I ran to the first man I could reach.

"Young lady, are you all right?"

I didn't even answer his question. There wasn't enough time. "There's a storm coming. You have to tell Lieutenant Crophaven."

"Hold on, now. We'll get you all checked out first."

"No, we need to evac!" I tugged on his bio-suit. "The storm will bring the same thing that made Ray and Amber sick."

His eyes flitted sideways to the rest of the rescue team.

"She's right," Corvus said. "If we don't get out of here, we're all going to get sick." Alcor and Lyra also persisted. I glanced at Nova, but her lips remained sealed. *Cold-hearted witch.*

The rescuer nodded to another man.

"We should get out of here before the storm hits, either way," his colleague suggested.

He nodded. "Okay, let's go."

"Send a message to Lieutenant Crophaven to evac the colony." I eyed his locator. The screen lay blank. They'd have to try the radio onboard.

"Will do, miss." He nodded. "Follow me."

They shuffled us into Corsairs, separating our group. Corvus helped Lyra onto a pulley while a member of the search-and-rescue team pulled me to the nearest ship.

"Wait!" I fought against him. "I want to be with Corvus."

"We're all going to the same place." The man pulled me ahead. "We have to get you out of here."

"Corvus!" I yelled his name, and he looked up and waved. "I want to go with you."

"Climb." The man instructed. "If what you say is true, then we don't have much time."

Tears stung my eyes as I grabbed the ladder and took the first step up. Nova gave me a shove to get going and once again I cursed all the reasons why fate stuck me with her yet again. Gritting my teeth, I climbed aboard and sat in the last row, slumping down into my seat restraints.

Nova took the seat across from me. "When we get back, I'm reporting you."

Exhaustion consumed my anger, and all I could do was shrug. "Go ahead. Have fun."

I closed my eyes to shut her out and sat back, hoping nothing happened to Corvus's ship. The engines flared up, rumbling my empty stomach. My mission had come to an end, and I'd achieved everything I wanted. I'd saved Sirius and his crew, found the plant field behind the ridge, and informed the colony. I'd fulfilled Great-grandma Tiff's expectations. Yet hollowness filled my body. So many problems were still unresolved. I'd told Sirius my true feelings, but Corvus had no idea.

A voice spoke on the intercom. "Prepare for takeoff."

Footsteps sounded past me, but I didn't open my eyes. I was sick of drama and couldn't deal with Nova anymore. A familiar voice whispered in my ear.

"I heard what you told Sirius in the Landrover."

My eyes flung open. "Corvus!"

He must have climbed on at the last minute. He sat next to me and clicked on his seat restraints.

I decided to confess everything. "I'm sorry. I should have told you. That day I bumped into you in the hall, I was running to my grandpapa to put in a request. I was running from you—"

He put up a hand to silence me. My heart clutched inside my chest and I thought I'd spew it out right into his lap.

"I know how you felt about Sirius when you heard about the match. It doesn't matter." His hand grazed my cheek. "What matters is how you feel now." His lips tickled my earlobe. "How do you feel now?"

I turned my head to face him and swallowed. "I want you."

He bent down and whispered against my lips. "I want you, too."

***

I roamed among buildings, knowing with a pang in my heart that what I saw could never be again. The towers spiraled up to the sky in pin-pricks carved from ivory. Aliens flew from window to window like angels with gossamer wings. They had a garden with onion-shaped bulbs swelling over crystal shards. Some carried eggs as large as a child's sleep pod across the ridges between the balconies, setting them up to sparkle in the purple sunlight.

Was I in a past time? Their time?

The sky cracked above me. Swirling storm clouds rolled over the ridge like planetary guardians, spitting forth their spite in rain. No, it can't be. My insides clutched. I reached up to the sky to warn the flying aliens, but no one looked down at me.

"Get inside!" I shouted so hard my throat hurt. But it wouldn't do them any good. They'd constructed their buildings with open walkways. The windows had fluttering ribbons instead of glass. Even if they all rushed inside before the rains came, the microbes could travel on the wind into their houses.

In that moment, I hated Paradise 21. It was more of a hell in disguise; a lure to trap innocent beings from other worlds and poison them once they established their homes. No wonder the planet didn't have mammals or any form of intelligent life. Here on Paradise 21, plants reigned.

A smaller alien huddled by the foundation of a building. It drew abstract symbols in the black crystal sand with its branch-like fingers, or fingernails—I couldn't tell where one stopped and the other began. I approached it carefully, knowing both of us didn't have much time.

The pearly eyes didn't scare me any longer. They glittered with intelligence and an all-encompassing sense of peace. The being scratched the shape of a pyramid into the crystals and filled it with concentric circles. Its wings glittered like seashells under water in an oily purple-pink hue.

The tragedy of the situation rattled my very core. Maybe I could bring it to a safe place. Maybe I could save at least one. I reached out to touch it, my fingers shaky and cold, wondering if the wing would be soft or hard.

Before my fingers reached it, a bird call trilled beyond the buildings. The storm had arrived. The aliens dove and whirled in the sky, scrambling in panic. Fear rushed up my arms and legs, encompassing me. I froze.

The rain came, pouring down from the black clouds in a thick ooze and coating everything it touched. I wiped my head and shoulders, but none of it landed on me. I was an onlooker from another time, another world.

Beside me, I watched as the small alien cuddled up, trying to block the rain with its wings. The ooze filled the grooves in the patterns it had drawn in the soil just as the rain washed the symbols away.

The planet couldn't wash them away completely. Amongst all the chaos, one alien stood upright while the others fell. He walked from the garden toward me in purposeful strides. I recognized his green-tinged wings from the greenhouse and the cliff by the ridge. Perhaps he had had the same job as mine, pruning the new plants to feed the colony. We were kindred spirits, even though we were different beings from worlds away.

His eyes beckoned, pleading with me, and I knew what I had to say.

"I won't let it happen again. I promise."

CHAPTER TWENTY-SIX

CHAOS

"Annie, wake up. We're here."

Corvus's kind voice interrupted my dream, and I awoke to the sound of engines as the Corsairs landed on the airstrip. I stood up before they flashed the seat restraint signal and shouted, "Everyone to the ship!"

"Hold on, Annie." Corvus fidgeted with his seat restraints. "The Corsair has to park first."

The idea of parking when the storm loomed so close was ridiculous. My eyes scanned the inside, and I wished the windows were large enough to jump out of. I shifted on my feet, feeling claustrophobic. "We don't have much time."

"I know." Corvus put a hand on my shoulder. "We'll be outta here in no time. You'll see."

The seconds it took for the hatch to open and for us to exit weighed on my nerves. When we got out, my eyes shot to the sky. Lavender-gray clouds gave an impression of calm above us, but in the distance, the black mass rolled in.

Engineers walked on the airstrip, tying down the Corsairs and covering the wings with tarps.

"Everyone needs to get inside the ship," I shouted, knowing I looked like a raving lunatic. "Forget the procedures. Run!"

My thoughts flitted to the greenhouse, and I wondered if Mom had received the message. I checked my locator, but then I remembered the crystals had ruined it. Where was she? Hadn't they told her I was found?

"Come on, Annie." Corvus pulled my arm. "Let's go back to the *New Dawn*."

"No." I yanked it back. "I don't think our warning was taken seriously. I have to go to the greenhouses. I have to check on Mom."

Corvus looked at the oncoming storm and then to the path leading to where Mom and I worked.

"It will take us twenty minutes to get there. What if she's already on the ship?"

A squirmy feeling in my stomach told me there were a lot of people outside the ship.

I looked into Corvus's eyes. "I just know."

"Okay." He secured his mask. "Let's go."

Sirius and Alcor exited their Corsair and I yelled out, "Spread out around the colony. Make sure everyone gets inside."

Sirius waved. Despite our disagreement in the Landrover, he'd follow my directions. Medics surrounded me, blocking my way. I tried to push past a man and he grabbed my arm.

"I have orders to take you to the emergency bay right away."

Before I could react, Corvus shoved him in the stomach and grabbed my hand. I stared at him in shock.

"Come on, Annie, run!"

We bolted through the jungle. Not only was it hard for them to track us, it was also the straightest path to the greenhouses. Thunder cracked open above our heads and fear welled up inside me, making me sweaty and feverish.

If I wasn't fast enough, history would repeat itself, and we'd end up like the aliens. That thought made my heart break all over again.

When we emerged from the jungle, two women stood on the perimeter, chatting as though nothing was wrong. They stared at me and Corvus as we ran up to them.

"Get inside the ship. There's a storm coming that will make everyone sick."

At first, both women eyed us suspiciously.

"I mean it." My voice turned to steel. "I know what made Ray sick, and it's on its way."

Their expressions turned from denial to questioning. The older one pointed a finger. "Wait. Aren't you the kids that disappeared a few nights ago?"

"You don't know?" I emphasized my words. The whole colony should have been informed of our rescue. We had found the missing Corsair, the expedition team, and sent out a warning.

Shivery fear crossed my shoulders. Unless Lieutenant Crophaven didn't get the message, or he wanted to keep it a secret. Unless he didn't believe us.

"You have to listen to me." I grabbed the older woman's hand. "The storm is coming, and anyone outside the ship will be infected."

She ripped her hand back and nodded to her partner. "Buzz Lieutenant Crophaven. Let's see what he thinks of this. Meanwhile, you two stay right here."

Like I was really going to listen to her? I gave Corvus a nod, and we both ran in the direction of the greenhouses. I glanced over my shoulder to see if the ladies were chasing us, but they stood where we left them, probably reporting us on their locators.

Corvus pulled me aside just as we reached the path to the first greenhouse.

"Wait, I have an idea."

I couldn't see how anything was more important than

finding Mom.

Corvus approached a box for the intercom system, and then it dawned on me; here was a way to alert everyone in the colony. If only we had access.

He dug in his pocket and pulled out his key tag. Thank goodness he'd taken it with him out of the Landrover. "Being head of security has its advantages."

I wanted to wrap my arms around him, but there was no time.

Corvus stuck the card in and typed in his access code. He pulled a small microphone from the inside and unwound the wire, handing it to me.

"Go on, Annie. It's all yours.

I froze like when I'd had to give a report in front of the class and everyone was watching and waiting for me to screw it up.

He put a hand on my arm and squeezed. "You can do it. Go on, tell them."

I took a deep breath and pushed my voice out, hoping it wouldn't sound too shaky. "Attention all colonists."

The sound boomed over us. I cringed back, but Corvus nodded and wiggled his finger for me to keep going.

"A poisonous storm is coming. It will bring the same microbes that made Ray Simmons and Amber Woods sick. Everyone must evacuate to the ship. Immediately."

My gaze went up to Corvus, and he nodded. He took the microphone.

"Code five-six-TRG-seven-eight-three. This is not a drill." He clicked the microphone back into the intercom box. "Good job, Annie." Corvus ran his hand up and down my arm. "They have no choice. It's the law: once an evacuation is called, everyone must go with it, even if it's a false alarm. Now let's go get your mom."

As we ran toward the greenhouses, colonists headed toward the ship. First only a few popped out of their work stations, then more and more funneled onto the path in an endless tide. Some of them carried important belongings and others ran with nothing in their hands. My announcement had worked.

A young man bumped into me and knocked me to the ground. I fell on my hands and knees, my right arm stinging. As Corvus helped me up, Mom stood with her back propped up against the greenhouse, balancing several containers.

My emotions came crashing down. I was so sorry for leaving. I wanted to hide in her arms and feel her forgive me. "Mom!"

"Andromeda!" She almost dropped the containers, but she had too much good sense for drama. She wasn't like other moms. Usually I hated her for it, but today I loved her even more.

"Ms. Barliss." Corvus took some of the containers in his arms.

"Annie, where have you been? What's all this? Was that your voice I heard on the intercom?"

"It was." After scaling the ridge, running among the pod plants, and coming back alive, I looked into my mom's eyes and stood up for myself. "I found a whole crop of those poisonous flowers over the ridge. Every one is filled to bursting with microbes. There's a storm coming that could blow them into our colony."

"Ma'am, are these really necessary?" Corvus pried more of them out of her arms and placed them on the ground. "We have to get to the ship."

"Of course they are." Mom glared accusingly. She picked them back up and hugged onto them like they were her children instead of me.

"Mom, you haven't been listening to a word I've said."

"Oh, yes, I have, Annie."

I paused because she never called me that. The nickname was a term of endearment, only used with friends or equals. Had she lost her mind?

"I've listened to every word of it. In these containers I have the antidote, the vaccine. We're going to need it if everything you say is true."

"Mom." I was almost speechless. "You did it?"

"I did." She winked at me. "With your help, of course. I was so worried about you. I'm glad you're back. I never want to lose you again."

Corvus was the only one of us with his brain not turning to mush. "This is nice and all, but we've got to go."

We distributed the containers among the three of us, me taking one, Mom taking two, and Corvus taking three. I was so worried about him, but it was the only way to get Mom to leave and not come back for more. Our burden slowed us down so much the other colonists ran ahead.

"Will they close the hatch without us?" My arms burned and I thought I'd drop my container and, with my luck, trip over it.

"They better not," Mom growled as she balanced hers and jogged.

We ran up the ramp just as a security guard rounded up the last stragglers.

"Is there anyone left out there?" I asked.

He scanned our locator numbers and read the screen. "No, ma'am. You folks are the last ones."

I wanted to ask him about Dad, but he pushed us ahead and punched in the door code to close the hatch. We were herded into the main auditorium. I ran to our pew in the congregation. Dad stood there, his eyes scanning the crowd for us.

"Oh, Andromeda!" He ran to me and flung his arms around me. "I feared we'd lost you."

"I'm right here, Dad."

"Where did you go? You've been gone for days. Are you okay?"

I couldn't answer. My eyes traveled up to the podium

where Lieutenant Crophaven stood in my grandpapa's place.

"Everyone settle down. There's no reason for panic." I could barely hear him over the crowd. The congregation had never been this rowdy before. People sobbed and shouted. He had to wave his arms to get people's attention, and he seemed more annoyed than ever. "Everyone, settle down!"

A thousand angry questions echoed throughout the room. He waved them back. "I'll answer all of your questions in due time. We'll get to the bottom of this. Who is responsible for the evacuation announcement on the intercom?"

Everyone fell silent. A mother shushed her whimpering baby. Fear spread all over me. I'd have to own up to it, right now, in front of everyone. Corvus moved to stand by me, but I waved him back. I didn't want to get him in trouble as well.

Nova climbed on the back of her pew so her head rose above the crowd. She pointed in my direction and shouted, "Andromeda Barliss, sir."

Every head turned to me. Their eyes seared into my body, and the condemnation hung over me. I stepped forward and nodded. "It's true."

A vein in Lieutenant Crophaven's temple twitched. "You breached security access codes and caused mass hysteria and panic. Do you have a valid reason for this?"

I gazed over at the main sight panel, but the storm hadn't come. In fact, there wasn't a drop on the glass. People eyed me with disbelief.

"I have reason to believe a storm of microbes is coming." My voice came out crackly and weak. I looked to where Sirius sat, waiting for him to say something about the ridge. His mouth was sealed shut and he wouldn't even meet my gaze.

What was I going to tell them? The ghosts of aliens

told me about it? Where were they when I needed them the most? And Ray? Why didn't he come out and show himself?

Because I was the only one who'd see them. My heart folded in on itself. Maybe I *was* crazy. I wanted to believe Great-grandma Tiff so badly. I wanted to feel important. I'd tried to save the colony and all I did was bring disgrace to our name. I was a big, epic failure, and they'd lock me in a greenhouse pruning weeds for the rest of my life. Boy, was Great-grandma Tiff wrong.

My voice shook. "Nova found a flower along with Amber and she brought it to me and my mom."

I looked at Mom and she nodded. Her unwavering glance gave me confidence.

"We dissected it and found poisonous microbes inside, the same microbes that made Ray and Amber sick. When I reached the ridge, there was a whole field of those flowers, and a storm was coming with enough wind to blow them right into our colony."

Corvus stood up. "She's right, sir. I saw the field with the flowers." He glared at Nova. "We all did."

Voices rose in argument. Some people yelled to get back to work, and others asked when the hatch would be reopened. Lieutenant Crophaven gestured for security guards to take me away from the crowd before I could bring any more discord to the colony.

Above the voices and all the shouting, I heard the pitter-patter of something falling on the glass above our heads. The closest people to the sight panel gasped. I turned, wishing for once I was wrong.

Ooze drooled down in streaks, blurring our vision of the coastline. It clung like glue and spread, working its way into every clear space, as if reaching out for us.

It couldn't get through.

That glass was so thick it had blocked out deep space, keeping us safe for a thousand years. It would do it again.

A woman's voice rang out. "By the Guide, she's saved our lives."

CHAPTER TWENTY-SEVEN

OFFER

I straightened out my uniform as I waited for guards to open the door to the main control room. I hadn't seen my grandpapa since that awful argument about Corvus and Sirius. I had so much to say.

A guard stepped past me and pressed the wall panel. "You may see him now."

Although I'd waited for so long, I paused. The culmination of the moment overwhelmed me, and my eyes brimmed with tears.

"Are you all right, miss?"

"Yes, yes." I wiped my eyes. "I'm fine."

I walked past him and into the sterile air. My grandpapa's pale profile stuck out from the chrome machines and my heart caught. His face looked skeletal and haggard. His cheeks were sunken in, and the harsh bone protruded underneath his thin skin.

"Grandpapa."

"Andromeda, my dear. Come in. Come closer so I can see you."

I stepped around the machines to face him. "I'm sorry I ever argued with you about the assignments."

"Pah." His hand rose slightly to wave it away. "I've been thinking a lot about it myself. I researched yours and Sirius's genealogy lines, and the two of you *are* a likely match. I can make the switch if you still want me to."

"No, Grandpapa. I love Corvus now. He's done so much for me. Besides, it wouldn't be fair. I failed the tests and deserve the position I have."

His eyebrows creased and a thousand wrinkles collected in his old skin. "Nonsense. What is all this about failing tests?"

I looked down as though he'd chastised me. "Dad always told me to study, and I never did. I was unprepared."

He shook his head and the wires rustled. "It's impossible to fail. The tests are meant to determine each individual's talents and to place that individual where he can utilize his natural abilities. It's not about how much you study, it's about finding your natural flair."

He smiled fondly at me. "That aside, you did exceptionally well. I have high hopes for you, just like Great-grandma Tiff. So far you've proven yourself quite the hero, or heroine I should say. It's time we moved you up."

"I don't understand. I enjoy my job working with Mom. I love Corvus."

"If you want to keep your match with Corvus, so be it." His chest moved as if he chuckled, but no sound came out. "As to your job, your actions have qualified you for a lieutenant training program, should you choose to accept it."

The room twirled around me and my knees buckled. I fought against it and stood straight. "I don't know what to say."

"You don't have to say anything. Think about the job

and make your decision in a few days. If you want the position, the training can start right away. If you want to stay with your Mom, you may. I think it would be a waste of leadership ability, though. The colony could use you in a more prominent role. Whatever you decide, I'm proud of you."

Somehow we were getting away from what I really wanted to talk about. Amongst all this business and all the titles, I still had to remember we were just two people: a grandfather and his great-granddaughter.

"I love you, Grandpapa. I want you to live forever."

He smiled, but his eyes were sad. "We all must travel this path that is ahead of me. It's a natural part of life, and I've eluded it for too long. Go on to the awards ceremony, but remember to always believe in yourself and your talents."

"I'll try."

I hugged him gently, fearing if I squeezed too hard he'd turn to dust in my arms.

***

"I'm afraid I'm going to trip down the aisle."

Corvus laughed. He looked *so* out-of-this-galaxy hot in his ceremonial uniform. His hair had grown out into a full head of blond curls, and I wanted to run my fingers through them and pull his face down toward mine.

"You climbed hundreds of feet, and you're afraid you're going to trip now?"

I giggled, which I never did, and took his arm. "Let's just get this over with."

"Whatever you like."

This time, his words resonated with meaning, with promise, over the light techno beat that echoed through the auditorium. It was the song we'd danced to at the festival: our song. I couldn't hold in my emotions. From then on, they were free-flowing, dancing to the rhythm of the beat.

215

I shook my head. "How did you do it?"

He raised his eyebrows. "I have my ways."

I took a deep breath and pulled him forward, proud to be on his arm.

The music crescendoed, the beat pulsing along with my racing heart. The entire population sat silently in their pews. Faces stood out from the masses. Amber sat with her parents, waving at me with her little hand. My mom's vaccine had worked and the antidote had killed all the microbes in her body. My parents sat together, holding hands. Their faces beamed at me, and for once I knew they were proud.

Sirius stood by the podium, waiting for us. Behind him, Lyra, Alcor, and Nova formed the back row. Lieutenant Crophaven presided over the ceremony. Medals of gold, platinum, silver, and bronze glittered on a showcase table, the metals a last reminder of Old Earth.

Lieutenant Crophaven's face was stoic. "We are gathered here today to honor those who saved our colony."

Yeah, with no help from you. I kept my mouth shut. He gave us the credit we deserved and that's what mattered. If I did become a lieutenant, I'd have to work with him, and I didn't want to spoil our relations now.

Lieutenant Crophaven clipped the bronze medals on Lyra's, Alcor's, and Nova's uniforms, stating their names to the congregation. Next, he awarded Sirius with the silver one. Sirius accepted his with a downcast face. He'd lost the confidence I loved most about him. Even though he'd broken my heart and offered his love too late, I hoped he could still find happiness with Nova. I doubted it, since she made a face like she'd swallowed a lemon, probably because his medal was *only* silver.

Corvus received a gold medal. When Lieutenant Crophaven fastened it on, Corvus smiled at me as though it was all my doing. I rolled my eyes. He'd done at least half of the work, if not more. After Lieutenant Crophaven turned his back, Corvus made a goofy face only I could see and I bit down on my lip to keep from laughing out loud.

Finally, Crophaven reached for the platinum medal. Heat traveled from my neck to my cheeks and ears and I knew my face was as red as one of Mom's humongous tomatoes.

"Andromeda Barliss, you deserve the highest honor." As he fastened it over my right breast pocket, he whispered in my ear, surprising me, "I'm sorry. I was wrong about you."

His apology shook my soul. Maybe he wasn't that bad after all.

I smiled at him and nodded to accept his apology. We turned to face the congregation. Thunderous applause rumbled around us. Corvus took my hand and squeezed.

I couldn't believe just a short time ago, I thought I'd screwed up a chance with the colony, a chance at happiness. It was even harder to believe I once thought living in the cocoon of the *New Dawn* was where I wanted to stay forever.

Paradise 21 really had grown on me. I'd grown as well. The sun shone on my back through the sight panel as if the planet had finally accepted us. As if I'd passed the test.

ABOUT THE AUTHOR

Aubrie grew up watching the original Star Wars movies over and over again until she could recite and reenact every single scene in her backyard. She also loved The Goonies, Star Trek the Next Generation-favorite character was Data by far-, and Indiana Jones. But, her all time favorite movie was The Last Unicorn. She still wonders why the unicorn decided to change back to a unicorn in the end.

Aubrie wrote in her junior high yearbook that she wanted to be "A concert flutist" when she grew up. When she made that happen, she decided one career was not enough and embarked as a fantasy, sci fi author. Two careers seems to keep her busy. For now.

Her writings have appeared in Mindflights, Niteblade, Silver Blade, Emerald Tales, Hazard Cat, Moon Drenched Fables, A Fly in Amber, and Aurora Wolf. Her books are published by Entangled Publishing, Lyrical Press, and Gypsy Shadow Publishing. She recently signed her YA sci fi novel with Inkspell Publishing titled: Colonization: Paradise Reclaimed, which will release in October 2012. When she's not writing, Aubrie teaches flute and plays in orchestras. She's a big Star Trek TNG fan, as well as Star Wars and Serenity.

Enjoyed This Book?

Try Other

Fantasy and Paranormal

Romance

Novels

From Inkspell Publishing.

Buy Any Book Featured In The Following Pages

at 15% Discount From Our Website.

http://www.inkspellpublishing.com

Use The Discount Code

GIFT15 At Checkout!

COLONIZATION

A DECADE SURVIVING ON HER OWN.
THREE DAYS WITH THE ENEMY.
CAN LOVE CONQUER ALL?

221

AUBRIE DIONNE

NEITHER CAN DENY THE CALL OF THE SEA,
BUT HOW LONG CAN THEY DENY THEIR
FEELINGS?

The world is about to be cloaked in darkness.
Only one can stop the night.

65395447R00138

Made in the USA
Charleston, SC
23 December 2016